Praise for
Violette Between

"*Violette Between* is a beautifully wrought tale full of characters that live and breathe. This surprising story from Strobel, a bold and engaging storyteller, left me sighing with pleasure and wanting more. She's not to be missed."

—CLAUDIA MAIR BURNEY, author of *Murder, Mayhem, and a Fine Man*

"Alison Strobel brings a fresh new voice to Christian fiction. Delving into the underside of complicated relationships, she takes readers to unexpected places but doesn't hesitate to deliver redemption when needed. She creates an interesting mix of unique but human characters—some that remind me of friends I have known. Good job, Alison!"

—MELODY CARLSON, author of *Finding Alice, Crystal Lies,* and *On This Day*

Praise for
Worlds Collide
by Alison Strobel

"I love this book! Alison Strobel has a voice that is relevant to today's reader."

—KRISTIN BILLERBECK, author of *What a Girl Wants*

"Interesting and entertaining; real and relevant. A captivating read from the get-go."

—PLUMB

"This is well-written tale."

—HARRIET KLAUSNER

A NOVEL

ALISON STROBEL

WATERBROOK
PRESS

VIOLETTE BETWEEN
PUBLISHED BY WATERBROOK PRESS
12265 Oracle Boulevard, Suite 200
Colorado Springs, Colorado 80921
A division of Random House Inc.

ISBN 1-57856-794-7

Library of Congress Cataloging-in-Publication Data
Strobel, Alison.
  Violette between : a novel / Alison Strobel.— 1st ed.
    p. cm.
  ISBN 1-57856-794-7
  1. Artists—Fiction. I. Title.
  PS3619.T754V56 2006
  813'.6—dc22

                                                    2005034191

Printed in the United States of America
2006—First Edition

10 9 8 7 6 5 4 3 2 1

*This book is dedicated to Gretchen Landon
and anyone else who has ever said good-bye to a spouse
far too early in life.*

ACKNOWLEDGMENTS

It became clear to me while working on this book that writing is not the endeavor of an individual, but a group project. Dudley Delffs, thank you for coming up with the approach that finally made this story work. Shannon Hill and the editorial team, thank you for polishing the ragged edges and smoothing the rough spots. Mom, thanks for being such an enthusiastic first audience—you always make me feel like a pro, despite how clueless I am! Don Pape, your assurance and encouragement gave me the confidence I sorely needed. And finally, Daniel, my best friend, thank you for your unconditional love and unending support. I love you.

$\mathcal{S}$ omewhere between the car and the gymnasium, Violette lost her burnt umber. She'd seen it while packing her supplies that morn-

ing, and after going back and forth to the house three times to retrieve other items she'd forgotten, she would have spotted it if it had fallen out there. She wondered if she'd ever be organized enough to keep track of her possessions on a consistent basis. She doubted it.

"Back in a sec," she called to Callie, the art student who was her assistant. The petite girl nodded and waved, then went back to mixing tints in paint trays. Violette retraced her steps to the car, making her way from the back gym door through the parking lot, her eyes glued to the concrete all the way. A few feet from the passenger door of her hatchback, she found the tube—crushed flat and oozing its hue onto the blacktop. Only part of her groaned in frustration; the rest of her had to admit that the swirl of paint looked rather artistic. With one last look at the abstract mess squished into the pavement, she turned back to the gym. "Oh well," she sighed. "A new task for Callie then."

"Your cell rang," Callie called when Violette walked back into the gym. With a sudden bounce in her step, she made her way to her backpack and pulled the phone from its pocket. She hadn't had it long and still thought it a bit silly; only three people had the number, and she was hardly the type who needed to be easily accessible. But knowing that Christian could call her any time he had a break in his schedule made it worth it. Sure enough, his number was listed in the call log, and she hit the speed dial as she rummaged through her supplies for her roller brush.

"Screening your calls?" he answered, voice teasing.

Violette laughed. "Yeah, this thing just never stops ringing!"

"How's it going?"

"Not as good as I'd hoped. Haven't gotten that far, and my burnt umber took one for the team out in the parking lot."

"Uh-oh."

"Yeah, but oh well; could be worse. How's your day been?"

"Depressing. Two couples bent on divorce and a third where the husband refuses to attend the sessions."

"Doesn't sound good."

"It isn't. Forget it, though. I'm bringing you guys lunch; what do you want?"

"You have to ask?"

She could sense his grin through the phone. "I assumed the usual, but with you I can never be sure. Burger Hut it is. Callie want cheese on hers?"

"Callie's leaving at eleven thirty. She has a class."

"Oh, all right then. Lunch for two. Even better—I'll have you all to myself."

Violette's stomach tingled, and she felt the smile spread on her face. "See you in an hour then."

Phone closed, Violette hummed as she pushed a new cover onto the paint roller and inspected Callie's mixing. "Looks good, girl. Do me a favor and pick up a tube of burnt umber when you come back this afternoon?"

"No problem. What do we do now?"

Violette shuffled back a few steps and eyed the wall. "Now we paint a mural."

Christian was still a new habit to Violette. It hadn't been that long since they'd simply been friends, and here they were at the beginning of a full-fledged relationship. She hadn't been looking for it—quite the opposite, in fact. But love did seem to be evolving. Sometimes she wasn't sure she even wanted it, but how could she possibly tell that to Christian?

No, if she was honest, she'd admit she *was* happy about it. Not so long ago she had been convinced she'd be alone for the rest of her life, and here she was a girlfriend again. No more meals for one, no more holidays alone—how could that be bad? Christian was good for her: steady but not inflexible, rational but not boring, mature but not stodgy. He appreciated her and her art, and the latter was almost more important to her than the former. She'd changed a lot in the last few years, but her deep connection to her craft still remained, and finding someone who understood that instead of merely tolerating it was easier said than done.

Violette was, in her heart of hearts, at her very core, an artist. Her love of beauty affected the way she viewed the world, the way she interacted with people, the way she lived her faith. The way she manifested her artistic nature had shifted as she'd matured, but remained her essence. She was no longer the quirky nonconformist who abandoned herself to every whim that crossed her mind or who deliberately adopted outrageous habits purely for the bafflement it caused others, but she hadn't lost all her sense of adventure and love of the unusual. It was sewn into the fabric of her soul. When God had knit her together, he'd used some pretty funky yarn, the kind that changed colors every few inches and had little wisps hanging off it.

Even though art was so integral to who she was, Violette almost hadn't allowed herself to attempt it. Her mother had been a celebrated artist in her hippie days, and for years Violette didn't even try to create in case she couldn't live up to her mother's expectations. Not that Sara DuMonde had been a pushy mom; she'd simply assumed Violette had inherited her gift for composition and saw no reason to leave room for the possibility that she hadn't. When Violette finally allowed herself to experiment by taking an art appreciation class in high school, she felt as if a volcano had erupted inside her: the images and ideas just kept flowing hot and liquid from her brain through her hand into the brush, the charcoal, the pencil. It had been such a relief to discover she could draw. She'd never forget her mother's face the day she brought home her first charcoal rendering: it was the look of happy shock that comes with finding a possession one thought was gone for good. Her mother was buried with that picture four years later when cancer got the best of her.

Being who she was made finding friends who would go with her flow somewhat difficult. When Violette met Alexine in college, she likened it to finding a soul mate. She was surrounded by artists—one expected it at an art school—but few lived and breathed it the way Violette did. Alexine had the same multicolored, wispy soul she did, and Violette was sure she saw traces of the sassy spirit she had so loved in her mother. Alexine became Violette's roommate, surrogate sister, confidante, and business partner. Between the two of them, they managed to get the rent covered and the utilities paid—although noodle cups and grilled cheese sandwiches tended to be the standard meal fare. They threw themselves into the starving artist role with abandon, content to skimp on what the world called necessities in order to fuel their obsession with beauty and art. Who said you needed new clothes every season? Who said three place settings weren't enough for two people? Who said towels were useless once they were threadbare? As long as they didn't freeze (not likely in Southern California) or starve, they could spend the majority of their money on paint and canvas. Both agreed it was the best investment.

College was eight years behind them, and still they both lived the life of the starving artist—although, by this time, the starving part was by choice. The opening of a gallery, Galleria Bleu, seven years earlier by one of their college friends, Xavier Thomas, proved to be the defining point in their careers, and after that they could truly claim to make their living off their art. They were no longer roommates, but their friendship was as strong as ever, tempered by the trials life randomly throws at people. One best friend was good enough for Violette.

Of course, now Christian had entered the picture. Significant others had walked in and out of their lives before, and each time Violette had to relearn how to share her time. Sometimes the intruder eased right into their little world with minimal upset; other times he barged in with all the grace and gentleness of a hippo in heat. Christian, thankfully, had been one of the easy ones. For one thing, Alexine adored him, taking pride in the fact that she had been the one to introduce him to Violette. The feeling was mutual, although Violette doubted Christian would claim to *adore* Alexine;

adore wasn't the kind of word he threw around the way Alexine did. Also, by the time Christian appeared, the women were in separate houses and on separate schedules; their lives didn't intersect as much as they once had. Sharing came a little more easily. But still, just knowing someone else wanted first dibs on her time made her balk just a little in defense of the other who wanted some of her too. It was the same part of her that wondered whether she should be in a committed relationship at all; life was much simpler when she was a loner.

She was doing her best, though, to open herself up to Christian. Most of her was on board with the relationship now; having eased into it with a friendship first made it easier to navigate. But still one corner of her heart remained guarded, refusing to fall for Christian entirely. Christian didn't know—she couldn't bring herself to tell him—but if things got any more serious, she'd have to say something. It wasn't fair to him that he wasn't getting as much as he was giving. She still held out hope that something would change for her, that she'd be able to wrench that last bit of her heart out of the past and into a new future with someone who loved her.

"I finished the edging down here."

Violette looked down from her perch on the top rung of a ladder. "Awesome. Thanks, Callie. Check for another roller and cover in the bag; you can start filling in the big spaces if you want."

"Actually, I'm gonna have to run. It's almost eleven thirty."

Violette laughed. That's what she got for not wearing a watch. "Well, that went fast. Have a good class. I'll call you if I'm out of here before two."

"All right. Laters." Callie tossed a backpack over her shoulder and went to the door. Violette watched her go, and then cursed herself for forgetting her Walkman. She hated working in silence; it was so unmotivating. She started humming to herself, and then singing out loud, taking advantage of the echo in the auditorium that made her sound much better than she actually was.

This would be the sixth mural she'd done. The first mural had been an Italian pastoral scene on her own bedroom wall; she hadn't wanted to experiment with a new skill on a paying customer's space. She had great fun with the Italian street scene in her favorite restaurant and a herd of stampeding mustangs on a high school's front wall. She'd painted a relatively simple mural in a local children's hospital hallway: a clear blue sky stretched above a field of sunflowers with children playing in it. And, of course, she had created the four-wall rooftop bistro scene in Christian's waiting room. That had been the most difficult project she'd ever done, and over the month that it took to complete, she and Christian formed the friendship that became the foundation of their relationship. She figured it was a good sign that he'd seen her at the height of her creative frustration—at one point she'd been forced to paint over an entire wall and start it from scratch—yet he still wanted to be with her. She knew she was not pretty when she got upset like that.

The first step in creating a mural is sketching out the big parts—this time, a row of knights on horseback whose shields spelled out the name of the school. It was easy in the sense that all the figures were the same; she'd just projected the tracing image on the wall eight times in a row. It was a difficult project in that each of the figures was nearly eight feet tall and three feet wide, so she would be spending most of her time on a ladder, something she did not enjoy. She didn't feel it would be right to make Callie climb up there—this was Violette's project, after all—so she let the assistant keep her feet on the ground and paint a three-inch edge around the inside of the sketch lines that could be reached from the floor. Violette did the same thing from the top, working down to Callie's space, then painted inside the giant figures with one color. She would paint the details over the single flat color, one shade at a time, until all the details were complete.

She had half an hour before Christian would come with lunch, but her stomach was already growling at the thought of the Burger Hut meal she'd been obsessing on. Her mind, though, went quickly from the burger to the person delivering it. Again, her stomach tingled, then dipped uncertainly, but in the end a smile spread over her face. She began to belt "Fever" at the top of her lungs as she pushed the roller over the wall. If she could get this first figure filled in by the time he arrived with lunch, she'd consider the morning a success.

"Fever in the morning, fever all through the night." Drag the roller through the tray, ease it back onto the wall to minimize splatter. "The sun lights up the daytime, the moon lights up the night." Catch a stray drip with the rag in her other hand, smooth the blotted space with the roller to even the paint. "I can't remember the next line," she improvised, then leaned to reach the edge of the figure and felt the ladder list slightly. She grabbed the top, trying to steady herself, and saw the tray slip from its place on the ladder's shelf. Dropping the roller, she lunged for the tray, then felt her foot slip from the rung. She screamed and groped the air for something to hold onto, but found nothing.

"Lunch has arrived!" Christian burst into the gym, paper bag in one hand and cardboard drink tray in the other. The wall opposite the door had oddly-shaped spaces edged with paint; he knew they were eventually to be knights on horses only because Violette had told him. He felt badly, sometimes, that he was so clueless when it came to art. He wasn't good at visualizing things that didn't yet exist. When Violette tried to explain to him a project she was working on, he'd nod and do his best to ask intelligent questions, but in reality he couldn't for the life of him see in his mind the finished product that Violette saw.

It awed him, though, to watch her work—to see indistinct shapes of color slowly become recognizable figures. He loved standing back and observing her; but he knew it made her self-conscious, so he didn't do it often. Or, at least, he didn't let her see him do it. More than once he'd peeked in the door while she was transforming his dull waiting room to a New York rooftop restaurant. Before they'd begun dating, before they'd even really become friends, he had taken every opportunity he could to watch her as she sketched or painted. He had such a respect for her abilities—perhaps because they were so foreign to him. Stick figures and geometric shapes formed the whole of his artistic portfolio.

The ladder was on its side on the floor, and it took a couple of seconds for reality to register when he saw Violette's motionless body beside it.

A foreign sensation like liquid ice ran through Christian's veins. He started to shiver. The paper bag dropped from his hand and the tray with the sodas splashed down beside it as he slowly knelt next to her. "Violette?" His voice was suddenly hoarse. "Honey?" His shaking fingers reached out for her neck, and when he felt the gentle throb of her pulse, the liquid ice warmed and he grabbed his cell phone from his pocket to call 911. The dispatcher assured him help was on its way, but the rest of her words were lost on him as he stared at Violette and carefully took her hand.

"Not again, God. Please not again." The words slipped out of him unexpectedly; his voice sounded unfamiliar. "Come on, Violette, open your eyes, honey. Be okay." Christian was hardly aware of what he was saying after a while; the fear that her light pulse would stop altogether if he went silent kept him babbling.

Time inched on as he waited for the sound of the ambulance out in the parking lot. He didn't know what to do; he felt lame just sitting there holding her hand, but he was afraid to move her anymore in case he aggravated an injury. He felt helpless, stupid. He continued to pray, chanting the same plea over and over: *No, God, don't let her die.*

After an eternity, the wail of sirens could be heard, and he bolted from his place beside Violette to open the door so they'd know where to go. An ambulance, squad car, and fire truck were parking at random angles in the nearly empty parking lot. Two navy-clad EMTs jumped out of the rig and ran a stretcher toward Christian, firing questions at him as they approached Violette. Once they reached her, he was commanded to stand back, and he watched unblinkingly while they worked, dying to ask questions but afraid to interrupt them. The rest of the rescue crew came in—some inspected the scene, others asked questions of the medics or him, some stood back with crossed arms and watched what was unfolding. Christian thought of how Violette hated to be the focus of such concentrated attention—just hearing him recount her accident later would make her blush. *Sooner rather than later, God,* he begged.

The two medics carefully eased Violette onto a backboard, wrapped a collar around her neck, and pulled plastic straps over her body to keep her still on the board. One medic began to poke and prod her neck while the other cut her T-shirt up the center and attached leads to her chest. A machine began to beep in time with her heartbeat, and Christian felt himself relax just a little when he heard the steady pulse. "Airway clear. Give me the mask," the poking medic said to the other, and an oxygen mask was strapped over her face.

"She's not breathing?" Christian asked. He felt like he was the one who needed the oxygen.

"No, she's breathing fine; this is just to be safe."

"What's that for?" The other medic had begun stringing up an IV.

One of the other rescue workers standing next to him provided the answer. "Just prepping in case they need to start meds quickly."

As the medic finished setting up the IV, the other began to cut off her jeans. He inspected her legs and then her arms with the help of one of the officers. "Just checking for any other injuries," they assured Christian. "Don't see any; let's get her loaded."

One of the firemen came up beside Christian. "Do you have a car, sir? If you do, we ask that you follow the ambulance to the hospital. Can you do that?"

"Uh, yeah, sure, sure." The circus began moving toward the door, and Christian waffled—stuck between gathering Violette's possessions and following the medics out the door. He finally grabbed her backpack and jacket and ran outside to catch up with the medics, who gently loaded the stretcher into the back of the ambulance.

"Beachside Medical," one of them shouted to him before closing the doors. The lights and siren were activated, and Christian was almost paralyzed by the sound. When the rig began to move away, he jumped into his car and left skid marks pulling out after them.

"Mr. Roch?"

"Doctor, actually."

The ER attendant smiled. "Ah, what's your specialty?"

Christian tried not to scowl with impatience. "Psychology."

The interest faded from the attendant's eyes. "Oh. Well, anyway, did you witness the accident?"

Christian huffed out a breath, sick of being asked the same questions over and over. He wanted answers. Tearing his eyes away from Violette's still form on the hospital bed, he turned to the doctor and told him what little he knew. "She had fallen before I got there. I don't know how long it was; could have been as much as half an hour, because her assistant was scheduled to leave at eleven thirty, and I arrived just before noon."

"Can you describe for me the position you found her in?"

Christian closed his eyes and took a deep breath. This was the scene he most wanted to forget. "On her back, head rolled to the right. Most of her was on the pile of drop cloths, but her head was just beyond them. Her arms were…" He pantomimed the angles, then dropped his arms heavily to his sides. "Please tell me what's going on. No one has told me anything."

The attendant motioned to a pair of plastic chairs and led Christian to one of them. Sitting in the other, he folded his hands in his lap and crossed his legs, as though settling in for a long conversation. No simple answers then. Christian braced himself for the worst.

"I have to say that her injuries—or lack thereof—are nothing short of miraculous. Typically with a fall from the height we're hypothesizing would have caused a broken neck or broken back— at least a broken arm or leg or ribs—but all we're seeing here is some bruising. Of course," he added quickly, seeing the light spark in Christian's eyes, "she has sustained a very serious head injury, and despite her well-being in all other areas, we cannot guarantee her recovery."

The colors of the room seem to fade, a film settling over everything. "She won't recover?"

The doctor shrugged. "Most coma patients, especially those with as little trauma to the head as Violette, will come out of the coma in two to four weeks. But then she could have temporary or permanent damage to various fine motor skills, memory, or even personality. At this point it's a waiting game. We just don't know when or if she may come out or what her issues might be post-coma."

Machine beeps were the only sound in the room. Christian's eyes drifted back to the bed, to the form under the white hospital blankets. "So now what?"

"Now we wait."

Alexine was standing at the front desk when Christian and the doctor emerged from Violette's room. Christian had called her on the way over, barking out only "Violette's hurt" and the name of the hospital. Seeing a familiar face brought Christian some relief; at least he wasn't in here alone anymore. "Alexine! Over here," he called down the hall. She smiled at his voice and jogged down the hall to meet him, but her hope visibly faded the minute his expression registered. "What's going on?"

"Coma."

"Is that all?"

He almost laughed. "*All?* Yeah, it is, so far; but trust me, we'd rather be dealing with shattered bones than this." He raked a hand through his hair, trying to hold onto his sanity. "They can't give me a straight answer on anything. No promise she'll come out of it, no promise of what she'll be like if she does." The crumbling look on Alexine's face wasn't helping him any. The shock of the news was seeping into his brain, displacing every other thought. Reality had completely changed.

Alexine took his hand, pulled him back into Violette's room, and ushered him into the chair he'd just left. Then she walked to the side of the bed and smoothed the sheets over Violette's legs. Alexine bit her lip as she glanced over to the machines beside the bed. "Oh, girlfriend," she sighed. "What did you do?" Turning to Christian, she asked, "So now what?"

He stared past her. "We just sit and wait." His voice grew shakier with each word.

"Did they say anything about how to stimulate her brain? Can we encourage her to wake up?"

"The doctor I talked to didn't tell me a whole lot. I don't know what to do."

"Not the type of work you psychologists usually deal with, huh?" She tried to grin.

A corner of his mouth lifted. "Not exactly."

"All right then." She pulled her car keys from her pocket and headed for the door. "I'm going to get some information. But first some basic needs. What do you want: lunch, coffee, candy bar?"

The word "lunch" conjured the plans he'd had for the day, and he groaned. "My clients."

Alexine rolled her eyes. "That's the last thing you need. I'll swing by your office and post a note on the door that you're out for the rest of the day."

"Week."

"All right then, week. But you haven't eaten, right? I'll bring you something."

He mustered a halfhearted thank you. She nodded and let herself out of the room, leaving Christian alone with Violette. After a moment, he stood and moved the chair to the side of her bed. Snaking his hand between the bars of the bed rail, he grasped her hand and tried not to cry.

Violette

*B*lack.
 Pain.
Cold.
Silence.
Sound.
A voice.
His voice.
"I love you, Violette."
He's here?
"You astonish me, you know that? You're beautiful, you're gifted, you're absolutely nothing like me...and I love you for that."
Where is he?
"Okay, I'll admit you drive me a little nuts sometimes. But opposites attract, right? Life is no fun when you're surrounded by people just like yourself. Variety is the spice of life, and all that."

October 1988

His face, his voice—piece by piece they fade in, surrounded by the trappings of a stark hospital room. I feel the sting of an IV in my arm, pain throbbing through my body. I am groggy, drunklike. He squeezes my hand, and I watch myself smile. My hair is disheveled and my face is pale, but he doesn't seem to care.

Strange that I can see that.

"You really had me scared, babe. Don't ever leave me, okay? I love you."

Oh Saul, I love you too.

A burger and fries had never tasted so bad. Alexine, bless her heart, had gone to the nearest fast food joint to buy Christian's

lunch. She didn't know he'd been to the same place just two hours before, that he'd reveled in the thought that he knew Violette well enough to know exactly what to get without her needing to articulate it. As he sat beside her now, listening to the machines that whirred and chimed and blinked, the food tasted like ashes.

After delivering lunch, Alexine left again, promising Christian she'd return with something to help them better understand what was going on in Violette's head. He didn't know where she planned on digging up this data; every spare doctor was working on clearing the traumas caused by a bus accident. None of them had time to sit with a grieving boyfriend and best friend to explain the ins and outs of comas. The sounds of crying and yelling could be heard down the hall; shouts full of medical jargon echoed off the walls. Occasionally the cacophony would make its way into Christian's head and he'd get more and more irritated that no one had moved them to a private room yet. But most of the time he heard nothing but the beating of his own heart and the instruments that monitored Violette's condition.

Once in a while the responsibilities that rested on his shoulders would come to the surface of his mind, and he'd contemplate them with detached consideration before tucking them back where they came from. He had six patients scheduled for after lunch today; so far he'd missed two and a half appointments. He was supposed to file insurance papers for one of his clients by the end of the week. He'd promised one of the elders at church he'd go over the new training materials for lay counselors in time for the course to begin two Sundays from now. The rent was due Monday.

He'd always been meticulously responsible, but for the first time that he could remember, he didn't care if the rent went unpaid, if clients got angry with his unexplained absence, if he disappointed the elders at church. He'd lost so much and stood to lose again—suddenly being responsible seemed trivial.

A slight smile tugged at the corners of his mouth. If Violette could see his predicament, she'd be amused. She seemed to have a talent for putting him in these kinds of situations. He was always waiting to see what would happen, one way or the other, with her.

Their relationship had been a seesaw from the beginning. For a man whose life had nearly always been predictable, it had been a shock to find himself attracted to a woman so completely opposite from himself. Violette lived in a predictability-free zone, where the normal things of life became unique and new.

He'd met Alexine first, at a local coffee shop where he picked up his morning fuel before heading into the office. She was talking to a group of women at a table near the register, and as he waited for his drink he overheard her discussing a woman who painted murals. Feeling guilty for eavesdropping, he interrupted their conversation when it seemed to have lulled and asked how he might contact this artist. Alexine wrote Violette's name and number on a napkin and asked what he had in mind. He confessed his ignorance about the whole process, remarking that he had recently acquired a new office with a drab waiting room and he thought a mural might be just the thing to liven up the place. She laughed at that. "If it's livening you want, then Violette is definitely your woman."

He tucked the number away for nearly a week before finally calling it. Never having known a real artist, he was afraid of what he might get, especially after the comment Alexine had made—it gave him visions of a woman flying in with crazy scarves and wild hair and throwing paint on his walls. Definitely not his style. Once he worked up the courage, he arranged to meet with Violette and review photos of some of her other projects before making his decision to hire her. Seeing what she'd already done might help him decide what exactly he wanted to do, even if he didn't end up using her to do it.

The woman who came to meet him the following week did not fit the image he'd conjured. Brown hair with a headband that pulled it back from her face, a simple blouse and jeans—no crazy scarves, no wild hair. She looked like a college student on her way to the library to study, not a professional artist. He wondered if she really *was* a professional.

They introduced themselves, and Christian thought he detected a hint of insecurity, nervousness. Understandable when meeting a potential client, he supposed, unless she was nervous because she didn't really know what she was doing. But the minute she pulled out the small photo album of her previous projects, all his apprehension about her abilities faded away. Her work was beautiful. Now he worried he wouldn't be able to afford her.

"So tell me what you had in mind," Violette said as she tucked the album into her backpack and pulled out a pencil and sketch pad. "This is a waiting room, you said? How big is it?"

"It's a waiting room, yes. Not that big, really; maybe…ten feet by twelve feet? I just acquired the office, and right now it's duller than dull." He smiled. "I'll be the first to admit I don't have a lot of decorating sense, but some places are just so plain lousy that even I know they need some work."

Violette chuckled and settled back in her seat. "Well, what kind of work do you do? Who will be waiting in this waiting room?"

"I'm a marriage and family therapist, so the folks who will be waiting will be couples, kids—whole families sometimes. All ages, all different situations."

"So we need something welcoming, something soothing—something stereotypically happy. Any suggestions? What would help people think of happier times and being in a loving relationship?"

Christian was impressed with her psychological approach to the project. He hadn't expected her to consider the people who would be sitting in the midst of the art every day. "Well, let's see…maybe something that looks like a family vacation? A beach? Disneyland?"

"Disneyland might be a bit chaotic—have you ever been there?"

"No, I can't say that I have."

She grinned. "It might be called the happiest place on earth, but the one time I went I saw more screaming parents and grumbling kids than I'd ever seen in one place. I think sticking with either a nature scene or something calm might be better. And it needs to appeal to both couples and families, right? We don't want to alienate couples who don't have children or make it something kids can't relate to." She began to drag her pencil lightly over the paper, making vague shapes and designs, then stared at the page and chewed the end of the pencil. Suddenly she sat up. "Here's an idea: Imagine the room as part of a restaurant—not a real fancy one, but nice and welcoming, and set outside. The furniture in the room itself could be similar to the furniture in the scene, to create continuity in the space as a whole. The other tables in the mural could show families and couples." Christian watched with fascination as she became more animated, sitting straighter in her chair and sketching in the air with her hands. "It could be a rooftop restaurant—I went to one in New York once. And at dusk, so the sky is all pinked up and pretty between the buildings." She turned to a fresh page in the notebook and began to draw quick lines that at first looked like nothing at all to Christian. He slid his chair over to the other side of the table so he could see what she was doing, and he was amazed to see a scene developing with just a few pencil marks. "The lower half of the wall could be a brick wall, with a wrought-iron topper"—he watched her sketch a rough iron design—"and one side could have a view of the Empire State Building." A nondescript skyscraper rose up in the distance beyond the iron. She sat back and smiled. "What do you think?"

Christian shook his head. "I'm impressed. I never would have come up with that."

"Well, that's my job." She bit her lip, then a slow smile spread over her face. "Oh, here we go. *Here* we go—humor me for just a second, okay? What if…" She flipped to a new page in the book and started sketching again. "What if we did *all* the walls? Stretched the scene beyond the room in all directions, made it feel a little bigger since the space is so small? This could be the side that faces west, so we get all that sunset stuff." She sketched minimal buildings, shorter so that the sky dominated the top half of the page. "And then the wall with the door into your office could be the building that the restaurant is a part of—like it's the door into the kitchen or something."

"What about the wall opposite that, with the door into the hall?"

Violette shrugged and tossed the pencil onto the table. "I don't know. I'll have to see the space I'm working with and probably go back and look at my pictures from that trip. I'll think of something. But what do you think? It's your space, of course, so you have the final say."

Christian sat back, studying the sketch and thinking. "Well, there's no question I love the concept." Violette's eyes brightened, and he felt bad for having to bring up the cost. "My only concern is that something of this scope would cost more than what I'd budgeted."

Violette nodded slowly. "That's true; it is a bigger project than usual." She squirmed a bit in her chair, then spoke. "But I'll level with you. I've never done anything on this scale before, so I don't consider myself experienced at it. Therefore, I wouldn't feel comfortable charging you my usual rate. I usually calculate by the square footage of the space, so I'll charge you half the typical rate, and if you want, you can even pay in installments if it helps."

When Violette calculated an estimate of the cost, he crossed his arms, considering her offer. Frankly, it was still more than he'd wanted to spend, but her enthusiasm and preliminary ideas were so intriguing that he didn't want to deny her the chance to put them into practice. On top of that, his curiosity about the project was piqued; he couldn't quite imagine what it would look like when it was finished, but he could tell from her sketches and the photos of her past projects that the result would be stunning. If nothing else, he'd have the most unique waiting room in the city. "Sure," he finally answered. "Why not?"

He thought she'd crow, she looked so excited. "Oh, fantastic!" she squealed. "When would be a good time for me to measure up the place?"

"Feel free to stop in anytime. I'm usually there by seven thirty in the morning, and my last patient doesn't leave until nine." He handed her his business card with his office address and phone number.

"Well, seven thirty is still the middle of the night for me, so don't expect me before noon for measurements. I'll draw up some formal plans and bring them over next week. Is there a day that works best for you?"

They settled on a time, and she reached out her hand for a shake. "I'm really looking forward to this, Dr. Roch."

"I am too—and you can call me Christian."

"Well, then, you can call me Violette. Thanks again for the opportunity." She closed up her sketch pad and stashed it and the pencil in her backpack. "It was a pleasure to meet you."

"Same here. See you next week."

Violette waved as she bounced out of her seat and toward the door. Christian watched her as she left; he was feeling strangely energized by their meeting and already anticipating the drawings she'd be bringing him. He hoped it turned out to be sooner than next week.

Violette

I watch from the corner of the room as Saul squeezes my body's hand through the bars of the hospital-bed railing. My heart soars. It has been so long since I've felt his touch, heard his voice—oh, how I've missed him! I don't understand how he is here again, or where I am, but I cannot deny that it is Saul before me. I can feel his hand, but oddly it seems smaller than I remember it. Maybe I've just forgotten; it has been almost three years, after all.

I've been here before. I remember the small paper Christmas stocking hanging above my bed and the vase of roses on the table to my right. But everything feels like some twisted form of déjà vu. Why am I in a hospital bed? Of course: my emergency appendectomy—now I remember. But why am I watching from afar?

I nearly panic, but then decide that as strange as the sensation is, I don't really care. The important thing is that Saul is back, here with me, holding my hand, and smiling down at me with those deep brown eyes that glint like sequins.

I close my eyes, wanting simply to revel in his presence, his hand on mine. So long—it has been *so long*. Memories of our time together flood my mind, and I run from one to another like a child on a toy-store shopping spree: days at the beach, vacation in New York, moving into our house, nights in the city. Then, suddenly, a dark memory flares before me and I gasp, panic rising. I grasp his hand tighter, afraid, and open my eyes. Saul's hand is cold and limp, and I scream. I am no longer in the hospital. I am at home. *God, no!* I drop his hand and clap my palms over my ears, trying to shut out the echo of my cry, and squeeze my eyes shut. *Anything else. Please, God, any memory but that.*

The pain and fear begin to slip away, and when I open my eyes, the scene is replaced by Galleria Bleu. Before my eyes, the walls of my own private room at the gallery materialize, and in the distance, growing louder, I hear the music of the string quartet we had hired for the grand opening. I see my canvases, painstakingly hung on the clean white walls, my artist information cards mounted beside them. I see myself standing before one of the canvases, staring with a critical eye at my work.

What a night this has been. I have imbibed a bit too much, goaded on by my nerves. Alexine and I have taken turns consoling each other when we second-guess our talent and berate ourselves for hanging *that* canvas instead of a different one.

I feel the energy of that night zinging through my bones once again. I feel lightheaded from the wine and excitement, chilly in my strapless red dress as the evening ocean breeze wafts through the door and caresses my bare shoulders. Before me is one of the largest canvases I've hung. I almost hadn't offered it to be sold; something about the piece made me want to hold onto it, even though I had nowhere to put it. Still, when my other self spies the sold sign taped to her info card, she nearly does a cartwheel, right on the gallery floor. She stares proudly at the canvas and I watch as a man sidles up to say, "It's beautiful."

Violette turns and smiles at him. I want to warn her, but I can say nothing. "One of my favorites," she replies. "I love the way the light filters through the branches." She glances sidelong at the man, sizing him up. I know what she's thinking of him: *He's cute.* No—more hot than cute. Dark eyes, sun-bleached hair, with an easy sort of posture that exudes confidence.

He flashes a smile, but then turns back to the painting and frowns slightly. "That is a nice effect. Not crazy about all the black, though. It's kind of…dark."

I feel the heat rise high in my cheeks and watch Violette's face grow red as she kicks into defense mode. "I don't think that's true at all," she counters. "The black provides a foil for the other colors; besides, if you look at the title, and maybe stand back about four feet, you'll see the purpose of the color goes beyond simply providing a contrast."

The stranger does as he is told, the slight frown not budging from his face. Finally he shrugs and stuffs his hands in the pockets of his dress pants. "Eh, to each his own, I guess." He smiles briefly at her once more before wandering away toward the other gallery rooms, leaving Violette to fume at the gall of such impertinence.

A moment later the crowds are gone. I am in Xavier's office, watching Alexine and myself hunch over Xavier's desk as he totals the sales. "Ladies, I believe we may turn out to be a success," he announces as he enters the final sale into the calculator. "I knew showcasing you guys would be the smartest business decision I ever made."

They toast each other with the remaining wine and sprawl on the folding chairs that surround the desk. "You'll never believe the conversation I had with one of the guys here tonight," Violette states after a few moments of silence. "He stands there in front of *Trees at Sunset* and tells me that it has too much black. Like, hello! They're *trees;* the whole subject is *trees.* Of course there's a lot of them!"

"I didn't think it had too much black," Alexine offers.

"That's because it doesn't!"

"Well, besides, it sold, so what does it matter, right?" Xavier reminds her. "Somebody obviously liked it."

Violette sighs. "I wish I knew who bought it."

"I remember who," Xavier says. He begins shuffling through credit card receipts. "The guy's signature was like a two-year-old's scribble; I almost laughed when I saw it." He pulls out a slip and reads the name off the receipt. "Saul Corterm. I'm delivering it Monday. Wanna come meet him?"

"Hmm. Maybe I will. I wonder if he's single."

Xavier sighs. "No wedding ring, but I could tell I wasn't his type, if you know what I mean. Unfortunate too. He was tasty."

Alexine pats Xavier's arm. "Poor baby."

Violette swings a leg lazily over the arm of the chair. "It would make sense, you know, that he'd be single. That piece was probably my all-time, absolute favorite; you know how much I debated about hanging it. I just know it was meant to be back in my possession eventually, and if this Saul and I hook up, then it will be."

I want to warn my doppelgänger that something is coming. I blurt out a nonsense noise just to see what will happen, but no one seems to hear me.

Suddenly I am in the truck with Xavier and Violette as they drive up Route 1 on their way to Saul Corterm's house. Nerves prick my stomach as I anticipate the meeting. I watch Violette fret over her hair and clothes and know she's praying that she'll make a good first impression. From the driver's seat, Xavier alternately teases her and calms her, and then they are pulling into the parking lot of a condo complex. Xavier points to an upper unit. "That's it. Number 56. Ready to meet your destiny?"

I watch Violette sock Xavier in the arm before hopping down

to the asphalt. It takes both of them to wrangle the canvas up the stairs, and Violette forces Xavier to take the front position because she's too nervous for the task. They ascend the stairs and rest the frame on their feet as they wait for the door to open. The face that greets them nearly sends Violette into shock, and I laugh out loud. "It's you!" she says.

Saul props the screen open and stares at her a moment before recognition sets in. "Oh, from the gallery; I remember you."

"*You* bought the piece? I thought you didn't like it."

"Oh no, I didn't say that. Just didn't like all the black. Loved the rest of it, though."

Xavier sticks his hand out to Saul. "Xavier Thomas. I own the Galleria Bleu. We spoke on Friday."

"Yes, of course."

Xavier motions to his companion. "This is Violette DuMonde, the artist of *Trees at Sunset*."

I giggle at the look of embarrassment on Saul's face. "O-oh," he stammers. "I...oh, I hope you weren't, um, offended..."

"Me? Offended? Oh, heavens no," Violette demurs, sarcasm coating the words. "Now, where do you want it?" She is clearly eager to get out of there.

Saul gestures into the living room, where he indicates a blank wall. "Just prop it up there," he instructs. "I really appreciate your bringing it..."

"Of course," she answers. "A *pleasure* seeing you again." She turns to Xavier and arches her eyebrows, a silent command that they leave, and then lets herself out the front door.

"The nerve!" Violette seethes on the way back to the truck. Xavier laughs quietly beside her; he is enjoying all this way too much, but she doesn't care. "'I hope you weren't offended,'" she mimics. "No, gee, not at all, feel free to rip into my art any time."

"He's not an artist, obviously; you can't blame him for being a bit gauche."

"Whatever. He's an adult, supposedly; he should at least have some manners."

"Easy, tiger, come on," Xavier coaxes. "Don't tell me this is the first time someone has bad-mouthed your stuff to your face."

"Just because it's happened before doesn't make it any easier," she replies. "And besides, now I'm never gonna be with that piece again. Mr. Art Critic himself will have it up on his wall, never really appreciating it, and I have to live knowing my favorite piece is being held captive by someone who doesn't get it."

I reach out to console this mirror image I am watching, but Violette doesn't even notice the hand on her shoulder.

$\mathcal{A}$ lexine came back a few hours after dropping off Christian's lunch bearing two books and a handful of pamphlets that she

proudly plunked onto Violette's bedside table. "Research," she stated. "God bless the Orange County library system and the hospital's information desk."

Christian stared at the stack without moving. He'd been craving *something* that would tell him what was going on in Violette's mind, but now that he might actually have it, he was afraid to look. He didn't know if he could handle what he found.

Alexine studied him, hand on hip. "Not what you were hoping for?"

"It's exactly what I was hoping for. Just not sure now that I want it."

She nodded and smiled sadly. "Well, it's here when you need

it. I'm going to take one of the books down to the cafeteria and get something to drink, do a little reading. Come join me if you want to."

Christian nodded and forced a smile. "Thanks, Alexine. I appreciate it. Maybe I'll be down later."

After she left, he stared at the remaining book and brochures and fought an inner battle over whether or not to look at them. Finally, after a few minutes, he grabbed the top pamphlet and left the room. He had to get out of the ER area, just for a few minutes—the chaos here made it hard to think. He wandered down the halls and eventually found himself in the main hospital lobby. A gift shop at the corner caught his eye, and he went in.

It was a small shop, not a lot of room to maneuver around the displays of figurines and cards and books. He took his time examining the stock, looking for something Violette might appreciate, but compared to her art everything in the boutique looked too cheap and cheesy. He was about to leave when a rotating wire rack of journals caught his eye.

Being a psychologist, he'd often encouraged his clients to keep a written record of their thoughts, especially pertaining to a particular event or trial they had encountered. Of course, he'd never taken his own advice, even through his own tribulations. But with the possibility of a lot of lonely time stretched out ahead of him, he realized this might be a good time to start. Here before him were four tiers of blank journals, some bound in flowery cloth, others solid colors or even leather. One the color of his childhood baseball glove caught his eye, and he lifted it from the rack for further examination. Thin gray lines filled each page, and the leather felt soft and worn. *Pricy for a blank book,* he thought, *but Violette would say beautiful things are an investment in your mental well-being, so why not splurge a bit now and then?* He took the book to the register, then noticed a small pen display next to the gum and mints. They were hardly masculine, but Violette would get a kick out of them: jewel-toned barrels and screw-on caps decorated with plastic gems. He pulled a blue one from the display and set it atop the journal, feeling slightly foolish, but who would know they were for him? It was a gift shop, right? Violette's voice teased him from inside his head: *"Oh no! A pretty pen! A threat to your machismo! Run, Christian, run!"* He snatched another from the display—fuchsia—and tossed it down beside the first in tribute to her. He'd give it to her when she woke up.

Oh, God. If she woke up.

His purchases paid for, he retreated back to the room, suddenly loathe to be gone any longer than he had to. He set the bag on the table beside the books and pamphlets, flipped casually through a few of the books—not allowing his gaze to fully rest on any section for too long—and attempted small talk with Alexine when she returned. She left at dinnertime, having made him promise to call her the second anything changed. "And make sure to read this stuff," she said, indicating the book she'd taken down to the cafeteria. "There's hope, Christian. I promise."

"That's what I'm holding on to, Alexine," he told her as she waved good-bye. He closed his eyes and thought of the hollow words he just spoke; they rolled off his tongue purely from religious habit. *Heaven forbid that you let go of hope, despite how sure you are that it's gone. That would be losing your faith in God, and we couldn't do that, could we?* Christian sighed. Another test of faith. Hadn't he passed the first time?

"Sir, are you sure you don't want to go home?"

Christian snapped awake, wincing at the kink that had developed in his neck. "No," he said quickly. "I want to stay here in case something changes." He ran a hand through his hair and rubbed his eyes. A glance at his watch told him it was nearly midnight.

The nurse went around to the other side of the bed and inspected the machines, then wrote something on Violette's chart. "I'm sorry she's still down here and not in a private room yet. That bus trauma really maxed out the staff."

"I understand."

"I'll talk to Admitting and see if we can get her moved."

"Thanks."

The nurse replaced the chart on the foot of the bed and left. Christian stood and wiped a hand over his face, then stretched and walked a few lengths of the small room. Nearly twelve hours he'd been here. He had paced the floor a hundred times, scrutinized every inch of the room, memorized the placement of every instrument and the contents of every glass-fronted cabinet. He didn't know how much longer he could do this, but he couldn't just leave either. He'd never forgive himself if she woke up and he wasn't there.

The nurse reappeared a few minutes after midnight, followed by two orderlies. "Found her a room," she said with a smile. "We'll take her up now."

Christian gathered the books and his bag from the gift shop while the nurse detached wires and tubes, then he followed the procession down the hall to an elevator. Their final destination was room 417, a proper room with decent chairs and a television mounted in the corner. The nurse and orderlies positioned Violette on the new bed and wheeled the ER gurney into the hall. Wires and tubes were reattached, and a new nurse was introduced to him as the one who would be taking care of Violette in the night hours. She left, only to reappear a few minutes later with a blanket and extra pillow. "I'll try to find you a cot," she said as she placed the things on one of the chairs. "I know you may want to stay for a few nights."

Christian smiled gratefully at the woman as she left, then pulled the chair to Violette's bedside and wrapped the blanket around his shoulders. He closed his eyes. His last thought was that he should call Alexine so she would know where they were, but before he could open his eyes to locate the phone, he was asleep.

"*There* you are!"

Christian jolted from his sleep and nearly fell out of the chair. "Alexine. Geez, you scared me."

"*I* scared you! Talk about scared when you go down to the room Violette was last in and see the bed made up and *no one in it.* I was nearly hysterical."

Christian slowly stood from the chair, his muscles complaining with every movement. "I'm sorry. I was going to call you, but I fell asleep."

Alexine sagged against the doorjamb. "Guess I can't fault you that. Any other news?"

Christian shook his head and haphazardly folded the blanket, then threw it over the back of the chair. "Nothing. What time is it? The neurosurgeon was supposed to come down at nine."

Alexine checked her watch. "It's nine fifteen. Good, I'll be here for it then."

"Not much for him to say, I think. Not a whole lot he can do." A shudder ran over him, and he pulled a hand across his face. "I don't know how I'm going to stand this waiting, Alexine."

Alexine wrapped an arm around his shoulders and squeezed,

then she pulled the other chair from the corner to the spot beside Christian's and sat down. "I called Xavier, of course, and Drew."

"Drew?"

"The pastor at Violette's church."

"Oh."

"He said he'd tell the prayer team and offered to have the meals ministry bring you some food if you wanted."

Christian shook his head. "Not hungry anyway. And not planning on going home much. I can live off fast food and the cafeteria; tell him thanks, though."

Alexine opened her mouth, then shut it again and stood. "Want a coffee?"

"Sure."

"Be right back."

Christian watched her go and sighed. The last thing he wanted to do was field visits from the flakes at Violette's church; he quickly prayed that they'd keep their vigil somewhere else and not at her bedside. The prayer was only seconds out of his heart when a mantle of guilt settled over him. What kind of self-righteous talk was that? Violette *was* one of those "flakes," and despite the eye rolling her church caused him, he had to admit they'd been a positive force in her life and had known her a lot longer than he had. God heard their prayers just as well as he heard Christian's. Maybe better.

A knock on the doorjamb startled him from his thoughts. "Hello, Dr. Roch. Glad to see they've got her in a real room now."

Dr. Stone shook Christian's hand and then examined Violette's chart. "Nothing new, I hear." He read through the notations that had been made since his last visit, then hung the chart back on the bed. "I apologize for not spending more time with you yesterday to explain what was going on. I see you've done some of your own research," he added, nodding to the books on the table.

Christian chuckled. "A friend of ours did, but I haven't read much. Honestly, I think I'm afraid to know."

Dr. Stone nodded and gestured to the chairs. "Here's what we're looking at..."

"Am I too late?" Alexine stood in the doorway, two steaming cups in her hands.

Christian smiled, glad she'd made it back in time. "Dr. Stone, this is Alexine, Violette's best friend."

Alexine handed over a coffee to Christian and shook the doctor's hand. "Nice to meet you."

"You too." He stood and offered Alexine his chair. "I was just about to explain to Dr. Roch what is going on, so you're just in time." He went over the same information Christian had been given when Violette had first arrived, augmenting it with more details and medical terms that did little to clarify the situation for either Christian or Alexine. The bottom line was that comas were complicated cases that the medical world had still not managed to crack. Far more shades of gray surrounded this condition than black and white. Christian found his mind wandering as Dr. Stone rambled on; it wasn't until Alexine asked a question that he realized he'd zoned out.

"So, what we can do to speed things up?" she asked. "Any kind of stimulation or…something?"

"Well, we're not one hundred percent sure of what goes on in the brain during a coma. Some patients come out and tell us they remember conversations people had in the room or that they dreamed just as they would have if they were asleep. Others have no recollection of anything going on at all. Sometimes we see brain activity stimulated by certain sounds, smells, and tastes; other times we don't. It certainly doesn't hurt to play Violette's favorite music, for example, but don't get your hopes up about seeing immediate results. But, if nothing else, it provides you with something to do so you don't feel helpless.

"A coma patient's muscles will atrophy if left immobile for too long, so a physical therapist will be coming in to show you what to do to help her retain muscle mass and strength. The IV drips we hook up will provide her with sustenance, and she'll occasionally be repositioned to prohibit the formation of bedsores. She's breathing on her own, but we keep her on a machine in case that changes. Either myself or Dr. Gray will be in every morning and evening to check her chart and answer any questions you have, and the nurses will check her drips and readouts a few times a day."

He leaned back against the cabinets and folded his arms over his chest. "I think that about covers it. Do you have any questions?"

Christian shook his head. "Once all that sinks in, I'll probably have hundreds, but at this point, no. Alexine?"

"Same here. Thanks for the information, though."

"Of course. I'll be back tonight around dinnertime, but don't feel like you have to stay. I know it can be hard to leave—you want to be here in case she wakes up, I'm sure—but you'll go crazy if you're here day after day. Don't neglect yourself, okay? If/when she wakes up, you'll need to be at the top of your game to help her with the rest of her recovery." He pushed away from the cabinets and shook their hands again, then left them alone to contemplate what he'd said.

Alexine sipped her coffee. "Well."

"Yeah."

Alexine propped her chin in her hand. "Why don't you go home and take a shower? Or a nap. I can stay."

"No, not yet. But if you really can stay, I think I'll go take a walk."

"Of course."

"You need anything?"

"I'm all set. I stashed some food in my purse before I came."

Christian gave her a quick hug. "I'll be back in a while." He was halfway out the door when he backtracked and grabbed the gift-shop bag from the table. "See you later."

The hospital was technically Catholic, so he figured it had a chapel. Sure enough, after taking an elevator to the main floor, he followed the signs in the ground floor lobby to the chapel. The small room had stained-glass windows and dark pews. A beautiful carved altar was at the front, covered with a tapestry and adorned with candles. Not quite his comfort zone—his church was far less ornate—but plenty good for what he needed: peace and quiet. A couple sat together in the first row of the right-hand side, so Christian slid into a back pew where some light was filtering in through a window depicting a woman washing Jesus's feet. Trying not to let the paper rustle too much, he pulled the journal and the blue pen from the bag, then set it beside him. The binding of the book cracked slightly as he opened the cover, and the white page with its gray lines stared out at him. Now what? He was momentarily horrified at the advice he'd been so flippantly dispensing to his clients all these years. How could he suggest they subject themselves to a blank page with no other instructions than to write what they were thinking? He definitely needed to start giving them some prompts, or at least more direction than what he'd given in the past. If he himself couldn't figure out how to start, how could he expect them to?

With a slow twist, he removed the cap from the pen and poised it above the paper. His hand was shaking. He wondered how Violette brought herself to put that first dab of paint on a white canvas. He should have bought a pencil and not a pen. "Oh, for Pete's sake," he muttered. "Just *write*."

August 5

Well, that was a start. At least something was on the page now.
He cracked his knuckles and cringed when the sound echoed
throughout the chapel. What next? *Dear Diary?* Not quite how he
envisioned men his age approaching the whole journaling thing.
But he couldn't just start writing to no one. He chewed his lip, staring at the altar at the front of the room. His mother had journaled
her prayers every morning when he was a child, and when he'd
snuck a peek once at her spiral notebook, he'd seen each page
headed *Dear Lord,* which made him wonder if she was actually
praying every time she sighed the phrase upon discovering something that exasperated her. He jabbed the pen to the paper and
began again to write.

Dear God,

So what's the deal, putting me through something like this
again? I'm so angry at you for dangling another loss in front
of me. I really love her, you know? She loves you, she follows you, so why are you making things so difficult?

Christian looked at the page and blinked in surprise. He hadn't
expected that to come out. But it was true, every word. Suddenly
he was itching to write.

God, look, if this is your way of trying to teach me something, or punish me, or whatever, please don't make Violette suffer because of it. That's just not fair. Whatever it is you want me to get out of this, I promise I will. I'll do whatever you want—just please make Violette okay.

God, I really do love her. She's so unique. I can't believe I'm even attracted to her sometimes; she's just so different from me. And I can't believe she's attracted to me—for the same reason! I feel like I'm boredom incarnate when I'm with her; what on earth does she see in me?

She is, in nearly every way, the exact polar opposite of Cynthia. How I could love such completely different women, I don't know. I guess it sort of shoots the whole "types" idea, huh? Unless I'm the relational equivalent of blood type O—I'm universal, I go with anyone.

Violette, on the other hand, seems to be following a trend. From what I understand, Saul and I are pretty similar. The left-brain jobs, the strait-laced lives. I think he was even Presbyterian. It makes me worry, sometimes, that she doesn't really love me—she just loves who I remind her of. I don't want to be a replacement model.

Christian's sight blurred as his eyes unfocused. Apparently he had more in him than he thought. He put down the pen and rubbed his hand, rereading his words and letting his mind wander.

His thoughts landed on a conversation he and Violette had during one of the nights she was working on the mural in his waiting room. He remembered staying later than usual that night—his curiosity got the better of him, and he puttered around in his office until almost ten thirty to allow Violette to get started. Then he walked into the waiting room and found it transformed into a small-scale disaster area. The furniture was pushed away from one wall and covered with plastic; painting implements lay scattered all over the floor: paint trays, paint cans, paint brushes, blue tape, paint rags. Violette stood at one end of the wall, brush poised an inch from the surface with some dark color on the end. "Late night?" she asked.

"Yeah, yeah, late night." He made his way to the door that led to the hall and paused before leaving. "Got everything you need?"

"Sure do. Thanks."

"Of course." It looked like she was going to wait for him to leave before she started. He was disappointed. Maybe if he just asked. "Mind if I watch?"

Her eyebrows arched and she shrugged. "No, I guess not. Will you analyze my every move?"

Christian laughed and sank into a chair near the door. "No, I promise. I'm just curious; I've never watched an artist work before."

"Well, I can't guarantee it'll be the most exciting process. I'm just edging the shapes now so I can lay down the larger areas later with a bigger brush." She finally pulled the brush along the wall in a curving motion. "Once that's done and I finish getting the background down, I'll start working on the details—the chairs and tables, the people, all that stuff." She dabbed the brush into a can in her hand and blew a strand of hair from her face. "So how long have you been a therapist?"

"Eight years."

"You like it?"

"Yeah, I love it." The answer came too quickly, and Violette smiled and raised an eyebrow at him over her shoulder. "Okay," he conceded. "I don't always love it. I like helping people. But I get very frustrated with people who don't realize what they have and take their partner for granted."

Violette nodded, her ponytail bobbing. "I know what that feels like."

"Yeah?"

"Oh yeah." More strokes with the brush. "So, you married?"

"Um...no."

"Huh, a relational therapist..."

"...who isn't married. Yeah, I've heard that before."

Violette threw him an apologetic look. "Sorry. Totally not my business."

Christian waved his hand. "Don't worry about it. I *was* married, for eight years. But she died of cancer six years ago."

Violette's shoulders slumped and the brush came down from

the wall as she turned to face him. "I'm so sorry. I wouldn't have said anything if I'd known."

"Really, it's not a big deal."

"Of *course* it's a big deal." She turned back to the wall, but Christian didn't miss the blush in her cheeks. "Way to stick your foot in it, Vi," she muttered.

He couldn't help but laugh. "Ease up on yourself. You didn't know. How about you? You married?"

"Was. He died too. Couple years ago. Undetected heart defect."

"I'm so sorry."

She flashed him a half grin. "At least we understand each other, eh?"

"That's true. I'll never try to set you up with someone so you can 'move on.'"

"And I'll never introduce you as, 'My friend, Christian, the one whose wife died.'"

He laughed. "People can be so thoughtless sometimes, can't they?"

"Tell me about it." She began to outline another shape further down on the wall. "So did you counsel yourself through your loss?"

"No. At least, not consciously. Just muddled my way through. Did you go to a therapist?"

Violette laughed. "Ah...no. I went to bed."

"Went to bed?"

"Yeah. For six months."

"You're serious."

"Oh yes. Ask Alexine." She looked back at him, eyes twinkling. "Bet you're wondering about my sanity now."

"Only a little."

She shook her paintbrush at him, a grin pulling at the corners of her mouth. "Bet you're also wishing you could have done the same thing."

"I can't deny that."

"That's the beauty of being an artist. I didn't have to go to work. The pieces I already had displayed at my friend's gallery kept selling, and I had enough in savings that I could afford to disappear for a while."

"So what made you get up?"

"Alexine and Xavier. He's the one who owns the gallery. And my friends from church. They all decided it was time for me to rejoin the human race; and while I didn't exactly agree with them, I was getting awfully tired of my bedroom."

"What did they do?"

Violette paused to dab at a drip with a paint rag. "Well, let's see. Alexine and X gave my studio a makeover. That's where Saul had died and I couldn't bear—" she tilted her head and sighed. "Anyway, they redid the studio. And some of the folks from church would come over to hang out in the living room. They never tried to get me to come join them; they'd just pray for me, or watch movies on my TV, or play board games. Sometimes someone would bring a guitar and they'd sing worship songs, or any songs at all. Sounded like summer camp. Anyway, I eventually couldn't stand being out of the loop, so I started coming down the hall and sitting on the other side of the wall, listening. One day I couldn't bear being by myself any longer when they were having so much fun, and I finally joined them."

"And you were back in the human race?"

"Well, not entirely. I still didn't leave the house for a month after that. But they kept coming, kept hanging out, kept praying for me and over me, and kept cooking for me. I guess I went along with them more out of obligation—they'd done all this for me, how could I not give them what they wanted? But hey, it got me out and back into the world, so it was worth it, right?"

"Creative, if nothing else."

"True. How about you?"

"What about me?"

"How did you get through the grief?"

Christian never enjoyed being on this side of personal questions. He was much more comfortable being the interviewer. "Well, um...I don't know. I just...did. Cynthia was diagnosed with liver cancer, but by the time they found it, it was too late to do anything because it had spread so far. So we knew what was coming. Three months later she was gone."

"You're lucky you could prepare."

"Yeah."

"And what did you do after she died?"

He squirmed in his seat. "Took a couple weeks off work, went back to my parents' place in Michigan for a while, then just got on with life. I didn't know what else to do. I moved out here a couple months ago to take over this practice for a friend who was retiring and…here I am."

"Sounds lonely."

"It was, a little, but not bad. I wouldn't have known what to do if my friends had filled my house like yours did. I just wanted to be alone. Some of the folks from our church came over, dropped off meals, that sort of thing, but we weren't that involved. Plus we didn't know a lot of people there, so it would have been more awkward for me than helpful if they'd done more than that."

Violette finished edging another shape and sat on the floor to refill the cup from a can near her knee. "Well, I guess God knew what we each needed, huh? If no one had come over, I probably would still be in bed." She smiled and pushed herself back up to her feet. "Sounds like you and—Cynthia, was it?—shared the same faith. That's really fortunate. Saul and I weren't quite there."

"How do you mean?"

She chuckled. "Well…I think we both agreed on the fundamentals. Eventually, anyway. I didn't really believe anything until the year before he was gone. Alexine and I submitted some pieces for a local artist exhibit the Church in the Canyon was hosting, and then I started going because the people were so fun. I went purely for social reasons for a number of months. I met a ton of people and enjoyed the services, because they were very experiential and"—she paused in her painting to flutter her hands in a swirly way—"you know, touchy-feely, highly spontaneous, lots of candles and art and music and ambiance…the perfect church for an artist."

Violette scratched her forehead, leaving a smudge of paint behind. "Saul had been raised in a much more traditional church, with pews and hymnals and robes and all. He wasn't going when we first met, but when I started going to CitC, it sort of kick-started him to go to church again too. But he thought Church in the Canyon was flaky; he didn't trust the theology, although he was never able to give me a good reason why. I think it was just way too out there for him. Not a lot of computer engineers attended CitC; not so much up their alley, I guess." She stood back to examine her work on the wall, then moved down to the next shape. "So anyway, I didn't really go in for all of the spiritual stuff until Saul died and the folks from CitC started coming over and hanging out in my living room. It just seemed like they had something deeper going on than I did, and after a while I started asking some questions. I became a Christian about four months later." She placed the final dab on the wall and lowered herself to the floor to take a break. "So what's your story?"

"My story?"

"Yeah, your spiritual story."

This woman had a knack for asking all the questions he didn't want to answer. "Well, let's just say I think I would have been more comfortable at Saul's church."

Violette laughed.

"No offense meant to you and CitC, of course. Cynthia and I were much more traditional too, you might say. She was a good Southern girl, raised in the kind of church where the women wear hats and dresses every week and the men wear suits and ties. My church growing up wasn't quite as conservative, but it was along the same lines."

"So where do you go now?"

"Now?"

"Yeah, what church are you at now?"

Christian wished she'd keep painting and stop looking at him while they talked. This was getting uncomfortable. "Well, I've only been out here for a couple of months, you know; I haven't really gotten around to finding a place yet."

Violette nodded and tucked a stray lock behind her ear. "That's understandable. At least your faith was already intact when you lost Cynthia. I think things would have been a lot easier for me if I'd had that supernatural strength at the time instead of after the fact."

He refrained from correcting her. His faith hadn't helped him at all.

Christian looked around the little chapel and realized the couple in the front had left and an old man was just shuffling into a pew halfway down the aisle. He wondered how long he'd been there. The journal was still open on his lap, the pen still uncapped and prepped for writing.

I blamed you for Cynthia's death, God. We both know that. I don't know if it's true or not, if you really are the one at fault, but that's what it felt like. I'm not even sure if I've forgiven you. Is that why this is happening now? Seems like an awfully cruel way to motivate me. Just remember that I looked for you when Cynthia died; I waited for you to take away that pain. But nothing happened. It just got worse. So, the way I see it, you didn't hold up your end of the bargain. So you shouldn't be surprised that I left you. It sure felt like you'd left me.

Violette

November 1998

The sun is setting over the Pacific Ocean, tinting the waves with dabs of neon orange and scattering blinding white diamonds along the surface. The air is cooling and raising goose bumps on Violette's thin arms. I see Violette rub a hand up and down her bare arm and watch Saul drape his arm around her shoulder and draw her a little closer. This is our first date, hard won by Saul after weeks of apologetic phone calls and conciliatory gifts. I had planned on ordering the most expensive dinner on the menu and telling him off at the end of the night, but by the time we finish our postdinner stroll down the boardwalk, I am surprisingly smitten.

I can feel the sand finding its way into my sandals even though I don't seem to be touching the sand at all. I am following Violette, but not leaving any footprints. Even over the incessant noise of the ocean and the traffic on the street, I can hear the conversation between Violette and Saul as though the words are piped directly into my brain.

"Thank you for humoring me," Saul says after a stretch of silence. Violette smiles at him, and I know she's feeling guilty for her intentions to snub him. "I've been feeling really awful about my uneducated remarks at the gallery last month. What would you say the chances are of me being forgiven?"

She grins and shrugs her shoulders beneath the weight of his arm. "Well, you know, it's not healthy to hold a grudge, so I guess it's really in my own best interest to absolve you."

"You're very kind."

"You're very persistent."

"You're cold."

She frowns. "I beg your pardon?"

"No, not like that. I mean, you have goose bumps; you're cold." He stops walking and rubs his hands up and down her arms. "Maybe we should duck in somewhere and get you a coffee or something. I should have brought a jacket."

I feel a blush creeping into my face and see Violette's cheeks begin to glow. "No, no, it's my own fault; *I* should have brought a jacket. But I will take you up on a coffee; that sounds good."

I know she is disappointed when his hands drop from her arms, and I feel her heart *thunk* again when he takes her hand to lead her across the street to a coffee shop. They settle into two over-stuffed armchairs by the window.

In a blink I am at my front door, watching Saul tentatively lean in to kiss Violette's cheek. She turns her face and meets his lips with hers, and I feel the electricity of their kiss…and now *I* am the one being kissed. There is no other Violette; it is I, *in* her, feeling Saul's lips on my own, the weight of his hand as it settles on my neck. I enjoy the heat of our kiss, the flutter in my stomach—and then suddenly I am outside myself again, watching as Violette grudgingly steps back, murmurs good night, and slips into the apartment.

The transition leaves me breathless; but now I am inside the apartment, watching as Violette collapses onto Alexine's bed to relate every detail of the evening. I long to be back outside, watching Saul, but I can't take myself there. Instead I listen to the play-by-play and ache to feel Saul again.

S orry I was gone so long." Alexine unfurled her legs and stretched in the chair beside Violette's bed. "Don't even worry about it; you needed a break. Take as much time as you need."

Christian's stare was stuck on Violette and the bed. The shock of seeing her there and what it meant was still so disturbing. Trying to snap out of it, he rubbed a hand over his face and forced himself to avert his gaze. "No news, I suppose?"

"Nope. Same old same old. What have you been up to?"

He tossed the journal and pen on the table, suddenly embarrassed by them. "Nothing, really. Just thinking. Hung out in the chapel for a while. Nice and quiet."

Alexine nodded and stood. Straightening her clothes and slinging her bag over her shoulder, she made her way to the door. "Think I'm going to go to the gallery. X really wanted to come, but he had a couple appointments today. I'll see if I can relieve him so he can come by."

"Okay."

"Can I send anything with him for you?"

"No, I'm fine for now. Thanks."

"No problem." She hesitated at the door for a moment, then stepped back to the bed, grinned, and squeezed Violette's hand. "Later, girlfriend."

For a moment, Christian stared into space, but his thoughts soon began crowding in on him. He wasn't in the mood to sort through them. Instead, he turned down the volume on the CD player Alexine had brought in and took a seat in the chair she had occupied. Taking hold of Violette's hand, he cleared his throat and said quietly, "Hey you. You should see the chapel they've got here; I think you'd love it. The stained glass is gorgeous. And the altar is really beautiful. I wouldn't have noticed those things before, but I do now, because of you. You've trained me well." He flicked his gaze to the hallway to make sure no one was watching him. He was suddenly self-conscious. "Have I ever told you how much I hate hospitals? I really do; they give me the creeps. But I'm going to pretty much make myself at home here for a while, looks like, because I can't bear the thought of just leaving you here alone. Silly, huh? Sometimes I'm not very logical, I know. Somehow I think that would please you." He smiled and laced his fingers through hers. "So anyway…I bought this journal. You'd like that, too; it's very sophisticated looking. Really soft leather—here, feel it." He grabbed it off the table and placed her hand on it. "Geez, I feel like an idiot, but it makes sense that someone like you would actually be woken up from a coma from the feel of soft leather. It just fits you, you know?" He stared at her, watching for some kind of reaction, not really surprised when nothing changed. He replaced the book on the table and took her hand back into his. "Anyway, I started writing in it with this really snazzy blue pen with little fake jewels on it that I bought in your honor. Quite the departure from my usual black Bic, huh? You've made some serious improvements on me, Vi. You should be proud."

The silence settled around them like a quilt; he didn't even hear the machinery anymore. He rested his chin in his hand, leaning his elbow on the edge of the bed. "So hey, guess what today is? It's the fifth. Now I *know* you'd be proud of me for remembering this, because I know what a sucker you are for anniversaries. Today is the one-year anniversary of our first date that wasn't a date! Remember? Dinner at Burger Hut to celebrate the completion of the mural. And you freaked out a little when I asked you to go because you thought I was coming on to you, even though I really wasn't. And then I got all worried that I'd offended you or something…man, you had me so confused in the beginning; I couldn't tell if you were coming or going."

There had been some residual winter rain that night, he remembered, and she almost slipped on the slick tiles in the restaurant's foyer. He grabbed her arm to steady her, and the look on her face had completely baffled him—she was either horrified or offended, and neither reaction made any sense to him. She said nothing, though, and he tried to tell himself he'd just misread her, even though she avoided his eyes for the next half hour. By the time they polished off their burgers and shakes, however, things seemed to have been smoothed over; and when he dropped her off at the office so she could pick up her car, it was she who commented they should get together again sometime. "Just because I'm done with the job doesn't mean we can't still hang out, right? Besides, we both need someone who can relate to what we've gone through, and heaven knows none of my other friends understand what it's like to lose a spouse."

He agreed and promised to call. Every day that he entered his office and saw the beautiful mural she'd created he'd be reminded of this promise, even though he couldn't seem to act on it. Truth was, he really wanted to see her again, but he couldn't shake the feeling that she didn't feel the same way. He could see how she might be the type of person who said things like that to be kind, so people felt wanted and safe, but who didn't expect them to actually believe her or call in her promises.

Being a relational counselor had its advantage at times like these. He knew that losing a spouse could cause a fracture in one's ability to relate to the opposite sex, that the widow might balk at any show of friendliness and misconstrue it as a romantic advance.

He knew that it might take time for Violette to feel truly comfortable with him, and he didn't want to push it. He wanted her to come to him when she was ready.

As the days passed and she didn't call, he found himself more and more impatient to hear her voice on the line. He wasn't quite sure why. Yes, she was a fun person to be with; yes, he liked the companionship of someone who knew where he was coming from. But was that really worth the eagerness he felt?

When he finally pinned down the other reason, he couldn't help but laugh at himself. Yes, she was attractive. And intriguing. Okay, fine—he "liked" her in the junior high, "So do you *like* her?" sense. And why shouldn't he? It had been six years since Cynthia died, and no one would fault him for moving on and finding someone new. He hadn't dated anyone since her death, so really this would be a good start for him, a good way to ease back into the dating game. And it wasn't like he was looking to get married again right away; as much as he liked Violette, he couldn't see himself with her for the long term. They were just too different. So it would be good practice, just hanging out, being friends, dabbling in the romantic now and then. It would be good for him and for her, too, he was sure.

Of course, none of this was going to happen if she didn't call and he didn't either. So finally he picked up the phone in between appointments one afternoon and dialed her number. He ignored the shake his hand suddenly developed and left a message on her machine in a voice that seemed slightly more high pitched than usual. He shook off the disappointment that she hadn't answered and brought in his next client, then spent the next hour trying desperately to focus on his job and not on whether or not she'd call him back.

Violette

"So this is what, date number three?"

"Four."

"Mmm, girl, you're smitten. Smitten kitten, that's you."

"Oh, whatever."

Alexine snickers as she mixes acrylics on a palette. "Look at you, you're all glowy."

"No, I'm not." But I'm smiling, and so is my doppelgänger.

"Yeah, I think you are. We could turn off the lights and paint by the glow of your face."

I watch Violette peg Alexine on the back with a wad of used masking tape. "Get back to work, sister! Enough of yer jawing." Violette grins wickedly and turns back to her canvas, now completely filled with an abstract calla lily.

I try to call out to her, to remind her about the date she is about to be late for, but neither she nor Alexine hear my voice. They both continue to work on their pieces, and both jump when the doorbell rings.

"Oh no, he's early. Our date's not till six!"

"Violette, it *is* six."

She rolls her eyes. "Yeah, but hasn't he heard of being fashionably late? Who shows up on time for anything?" Violette dunks the brush in a can of water and dashes for the door, leaving Alexine laughing behind her.

Saul enters, hands in the pockets of his khakis, with that smile on his face that always melts my knees. Violette runs a hand over her hair, embarrassed. "Come on in. I was just getting ready."

He smiles, seeing through her obvious lie. "Not a problem. I can wait. How's it going?"

"Not bad. I'm finishing up a new series, and the last piece is on the easel if you wanna go look. I'll just be a minute. Alexine is in there."

"Okay. Take your time."

I follow Violette as she rushes into the bedroom and slams the door behind her. She strips off her paint-stained shorts and tank top, then begins a wild rampage through her closet looking for the dress she'd been thinking of wearing. Finding it, she yanks it over her head, smoothes it down, and fixes the sloppy bun she twisted her hair into three hours ago. At least I know Saul didn't like me just for my looks—I was always half put together when we went out. "If he'd just stop showing up early like he always does, I'd be able to really deck myself out," Violette mutters to herself.

Now we're in the studio where Saul and Alexine are chatting. "Like it?" Violette asks, motioning to her canvas. "Or is there too much white?"

Saul rolls his eyes. "You'll never let that go, will you?"

"Of course not! I'm ready whenever you are."

Alexine wipes her hands on a shop rag and flops onto a stool. "Have fun you two—where you headed tonight?"

"New sushi bar in Huntington."

"Beach?" Violette asks.

"Is there any other?" Saul laughs.

"Uh oh. Gimme a second then." Violette dashes from the studio to the bedroom, hearing Saul calling out behind her. I groan, remembering the pointless habit I'd religiously kept up in my twenties. Why had I insisted on being so odd? Huntington Beach meant red, cork-soled wedges, which meant a different dress. Violette whips the dress off and tosses it on the bed, then rummages again through the closet for the skirt and blouse bought at the thrift store to match the shoes.

"So what's the deal with the switcheroo?" They were in the car, music turned on low and the sun setting to their left. "That dress you had on before was fine."

"Yeah, but I have this tradition with Huntington Beach. I always have to wear these shoes."

Saul glances down at her feet. "They're...nice."

She gives him a sympathetic smile. "You're a boy. You don't have to pretend to appreciate them."

He laughs. "Okay, so, they're shoes. What's the big deal?"

Violette sighs. "Okay, see, I bought these in Huntington after seeing them there for, like, three months. They were wicked expensive for my budget, but I really liked them; and after I got them I felt bad taking them out of the window they'd been in for so long. So I promised I'd bring them back to Huntington whenever I had the chance, so they could visit, you know? And the dress I was wearing wouldn't match them, so I had to change clothes, too."

"Promised who?"

"Beg pardon?"

"You said you promised you'd bring them back. Who exactly did you promise? The shoes?"

Violette thinks a minute. "Yeah, I guess so."

Saul eyes her sideways. "You're one surprise after another."

"Think you can get used to it?"

"I'll certainly try."

The sun appears to set in a split second, and I follow the couple as they meander up the beach on their postdinner stroll.

"So now where?"

Violette shrugs, then smiles. "I know, let's go back to your place."

"Why?"

"Because I haven't seen it yet. You've been to my place every time to pick me up, but I've only been to your place that one unfortunate time. Besides, I'd *love* to see how my painting looks on your wall. I miss it."

Saul's face takes on a look of trepidation. "Um, well…"

"Oh, don't have it up yet? That's okay; it's a big piece. I know what a pain those can be to hang. I could help you, though. I've done a million of them. We just need a hammer and some brackets—"

"Well, no, that's not the problem." He rakes his fingers through his hair, looking uncomfortable.

I grab Violette's shoulder and shout in her ear, *It's not a big deal! Don't freak out over this. It's not worth it!* But as usual she can't hear me.

They've reached his car, and Violette tips her head in curiosity as she opens the door. "Saul, what's the problem?"

He heaves a sigh, then closes the car door behind Violette and goes around to let himself in. After getting situated in the seat, he turns to face her. "I don't have it anymore."

Violette frowns. "Don't have it? What do you mean?"

"I mean I…I sold it."

Her eyebrows nearly arch off her forehead. "You *what?*"

"I… Okay, you see—"

"You *sold* it? Why?"

"I sold it to an art collector. A friend of a friend. Actually, you should be proud of yourself; this guy said—"

"You *sold* my *favorite* painting? And never *told* me?"

"Violette, honestly, I had no idea you'd be—"

"Didn't you like it?" Now I am in Violette again, staring out my eyes into Saul's, which are pleading for understanding. Anger surges in my chest and tears slide down my cheeks.

"I *did* like it, yes, but I bought it as an investment. I had a feeling your work would be worth a lot someday, and in the meantime I knew it would look good in my place. So it was a win-win, really." He is talking faster and faster, and as much as I want to console him, forgive him, end this fight a different way, I can't seem to control any of it. "And then this friend of mine came over to borrow something and had this other friend with him, and the guy went wild for it. Know what he said, though, Violette?" He takes my hands, squeezing them, trying to reassure me. I stare at our hands entwined in my lap, feeling my anger slowly reaching critical levels. "He said you would definitely be a success. And this guy knows his stuff, you know? He went nuts for *Trees at Sunset,* and I told him all about the gallery and the other stuff you had there, so chances are you'll get some more sales from him if you haven't already."

My voice shakes with the emotions that are threatening to choke me. "But you never said, 'Forget it, this one is mine. Go get your own.' I have two others in that series, you know. He could have had one almost like it."

"I…I didn't know that."

"You didn't care. You didn't really want it in the first place. You didn't love it."

"I did! I thought it was beautiful!"

"Take me home."

"Violette, please—"

"Home."

He lets go of my hands, and I am out of body again. Violette turns to the door, staring out the window at the beach—and I know she is feeling utterly wretched. The sting of tears is still in my eyes. Twice on the way home Saul tries to get Violette to talk; both times she ignores him and keeps her eyes glued to the window. When he pulls into the parking lot of her complex, she unsnaps the seat belt and lets herself out before he has time to attempt being chivalrous. *"Don't* call me," she hisses before slamming the door. I'm already inside the apartment when Violette bursts through the door, and we both collapse into bed crying, ignoring Alexine's concerned questions.

*H*ey, Christian."

Christian turned from the window and saw Xavier in the doorway, looking as always like a Calvin

August 5, 2005

Klein model. Christian had to admit he envied the guy's sense of style, no matter what kind of lifestyle Xavier lived. "Hey, buddy. How are you?"

"That's what I'm supposed to ask you."

Christian flashed a half smile. "You can probably guess."

"Yeah." Xavier held out a paper bag. "Chocolate croissant? Fresh from the bakery—or was, half an hour ago."

"Um…yeah, sure. Thanks." That was a surprise. A lucky one too; Christian loved chocolate croissants. "Alexine take over your appointments for the afternoon? She mentioned you had some."

"Yeah, she did. I'm sorry I haven't been here sooner."

"That's all right. Don't worry about it. It's not like she knows, you know?"

"You don't think so?"

Christian stared at the books and pamphlets still piled on the table. Other than the one pamphlet he'd leafed through, he hadn't read any of them yet. "I don't think so, but I guess I don't know, really." He motioned to the chair beside the bed. "Feel free to take a seat. I'm going to take a walk, if you don't mind."

"No, of course not; go ahead. Take your time. I'll stay till you come back."

Christian grabbed the journal and pen from the table, then headed for the door. As he left the room he could hear Xavier chatting away at Violette, apparently not nearly as embarrassed by it as Christian was. "So I met this *gorgeous* guy at the gallery this morning, Vi…"

Christian had to admit that Xavier had never been anything but nice to him. As a Christian he knew he should be just as friendly toward Xavier as he would be toward anyone else, but he always worried he'd misconstrue it as a come-on or something. Bottom line was, he'd never had any contact with someone like Xavier and he just didn't know how to act around him.

Violette had sensed his discomfort right away when she first introduced them. "He won't bite," she teased later when they were alone. "And you're not his type, so don't worry."

"I'm not?"

"No, trust me."

He was almost hurt. "Well, thanks a lot. What's wrong with me?"

"Do you want to be his type?"

He rolled his eyes. "I just don't see why he *wouldn't* like me, that's all. I'm a nice guy, right?"

"Yeah, but you're not exactly a clotheshorse."

"Well, that's true," Christian conceded. "He does dress impeccably."

"And there's that little problem of you being straight."

"But how does he know that?"

Violette laughed. "Because he can tell. He's had a lot of practice."

"Oh. I suppose that's true."

Christian smiled at the memory of their conversation. Xavier really was a good guy, despite lifestyle choices that Christian didn't agree with. He really needed to work on befriending him. Xavier was, after all, Violette's closest friend after Alexine.

Would he see any of her friends again if she died?

The thought came into his head from out of left field, and he stopped in his tracks. Why had he thought that? Talk about morbid. The last thing he wanted to do was think about her dying, regardless of whether or not it was a possibility.

He found himself back at the chapel, which was empty this time. He slipped into a pew halfway down the aisle and set the journal and pen beside him. Candle flames on the altar shimmied in the imperceptible breeze that must have followed him in the door, and he watched their dance with half-focused eyes while his mind wandered.

This was getting old. As much as he wanted to stay here with Violette constantly, he was going to go mad if he did. Being surrounded hour after hour by an atmosphere of death and sickness and stress so thick he could feel it was sure to take a toll on him. He hated the thought of leaving her, but he'd have to do it eventually. And besides, he wasn't the only one who loved Violette; he wasn't the only friend she had. Even with him gone, she'd rarely be alone.

But to actually leave her...

He opened the journal to a fresh page and uncapped the pen. He still had some residual apprehension about writing in the journal, but he plunged ahead anyway, trying to ignore his sloppy penmanship that marred the clean page and focus instead on the words coming out of him.

I can't believe I've known her for over a year! I can't believe we've been dating for four months. I can't believe she's been in my life for such a short time and might not be in it anymore.

You won't take her, will you?

That first date, the first real one, was one of the worst nights of my life. I was so sure I'd screw something up. I can't remember being that nervous with Cynthia, but then again dating was part of the whole college experience. It seemed like the obvious thing to do. With Violette, though, it was such a big risk. We had hardly anything to build on, just those few weeks while she worked on the mural and that one date-that-wasn't-a-date that didn't go that well itself. When she called I thought for sure it was to tell me to take a hike.

Two days after he'd left his higher-than-normal voice message on her answering machine, she called back. He had packed up to go home and almost didn't answer the phone, thinking it would be a client; when he heard her voice, he was relieved. They talked for half an hour before he realized what time it was. When he finally got around to asking her out, they had been talking for nearly an hour. By the time he hung up, he couldn't remember a thing they'd discussed, save for one fact: they were going out Friday night.

For someone who viewed this whole thing as a transitional relationship, he sure was eager to see her again. He told himself she must feel the same way or else she wouldn't have agreed to go out with him. Unless, of course, she didn't see it as a date. Hadn't they agreed it would be nice to have someone to talk to who knew what they'd gone through? Maybe she saw it as therapy, as a chance for friends to hang out, nothing more. How could he show her he wanted it to be more than that? He was beginning to remember why he hadn't dated anyone before college. It was just too stressful.

For the next three days, he racked his brain for ways to subtly show her he was interested. He thought offering to pick her up might be too forward, and changing the restaurant they'd chosen to something more formal seemed too obvious. Eventually he settled on bringing her flowers—not a massive bouquet, just a small one of gerber daisies and tiger lilies that the florist had already assembled. He picked them up on the way to the restaurant, and then arrived embarrassingly early. Not wanting to look desperate, he left the parking lot and drove around the surrounding area until he realized traffic was going to make him late. By the time he got back he was indeed ten minutes late, and he couldn't exactly explain why without looking like an idiot, could he?

Violette was already at a table with a glass of wine. He suddenly felt like a teenager, and an awkward one at that. He questioned his choice of clothes, his choice of flowers, his choice of restaurant over and over in the eight seconds it took him to reach the table. But when she looked up and smiled at him he didn't care anymore.

"These are for you," he said, holding out the bouquet as he took his seat. "They looked like the colors an artist would enjoy."

The look of pleased surprise that spread over her face made it worth it. "Christian, they're gorgeous. Thank you." She buried her face in them, then laid them on the chair beside her. "Gerber daisies are my favorites too. You read my mind."

All night he watched for signs that she might feel for him even a fraction of what he felt for her, but he couldn't read her. They talked easily, and she seemed comfortable with him—more comfortable, even, than she had been the week before at the Burger Hut—but she gave no look, no spark, no vibe that indicated she saw this as anything more than just friends hanging out.

As they neared the end of their meal, he started thinking of ways he could give her a clue as to what he was thinking. Just asking if she wanted to get together again wouldn't be enough; she'd have no reason to view the next meeting any different from this one.

The check came, he paid, and then there was nothing else to do but leave. He stood and reached for her flowers just as she did the same, and her hand was so cold it shocked him. "Violette, you should have said something. Have you been freezing this whole time?"

She straightened, flowers in hand, and an obvious blush in her cheeks. "No, no, I haven't been cold. I've been fine, really."

"But your hands are like ice."

She ducked her head, shuffling her purse and flowers as she turned for the door. "It's just my hands, really. They get cold when I get nervous."

"You were nervous? Why?"

She looked at him and he blinked. There it was. The look. She began to speak, but her words got lost in an embarrassed chuckle. Finally she just waved her hand in a dismissive way and shook her head. "Sorry. Being silly. Geez, you'd think I was fifteen."

Christian laughed and steered her, hand on her back, toward the door. "Hardly. You're far more composed than the fifteen-year-olds I remember." *And a lot sexier,* came the next thought, but he wasn't about to say that out loud.

Once outside Violette took a deep breath and leaned against her car. "So have you, um…seen anyone, I guess…since Cynthia died?"

"No, not really. A couple well-meaning attempts by friends and family at setting me up always failed miserably. You?"

"No." She swung the flowers slowly, thinking. "Never thought I would, actually. I could never see myself with anyone but Saul." She stole a glance at him before returning her gaze to the flowers. "I still can't, really…but at the same time, I'm awfully intrigued."

He saw the small smile creeping over her face and felt his heart pound. Christian knew he had to tread lightly; he didn't want to come on too strong and scare her off for good. He also didn't want to go home kicking himself, either. "You know, Vi, I wouldn't want to do anything that would jeopardize a perfectly good friendship." She nodded, listening. "But on the other hand, I'd hate to miss an opportunity for both of us to be…well, frankly, to be really happy again. Does that make sense?"

She was chewing her lip, her eyes on the flowers as they moved pendulum-like in front of her. Finally she nodded and looked at him. "It does, Christian, it does. And I agree. I'll definitely think about it, but I don't know if I'm ready—"

"That's okay," he jumped in. "I'm not coming at you with a

timeline here, you know? Just…putting it out there that you have an interested party."

They stood for a moment, the silence cut by traffic noises and cars in the parking lot. Finally Violette righted the flowers and gave herself a shake. "Sorry. Kind of got lost in my thoughts there." She heaved a breath and flashed a small smile. "This isn't any easier as an adult, is it? I thought it was only awkward back when I was twenty and stupid."

Christian laughed and, unthinking, pulled Violette into a hug. "Twenty and stupid, thirty and wiser, forty and over it—still hard, either way." He felt her arms wrap around his neck and felt dizzy. *Thirty-six and whipped.* "Dinner again soon?"

"Definitely." She hung onto him for a moment, then released him and unlocked her car. "Call me?"

"Sure thing."

She took another deep breath and sagged against the car door. "Thanks."

"You're welcome."

Christian stared at the page he'd begun to write on. Again he'd lost track of time; who knew how long he'd been sitting here. He shut the book and capped the pen; the desire to write had drained out of him. Instead he stood and wandered around the small chapel, studying the stained-glass panels and looking up close at the carving on the altar. He'd never been much for the demonstrative traditions, but on a whim he dropped a quarter in the donation box and took a small votive to the spot where the other candles stood. Taking a match from the holder, he lit it off another candle and patiently waited for his candle's wick to catch. It smoldered for a moment, wax dripping from the string, then flared. He set it down among the others, then knelt on the padded step and tried to pray.

Oh, God...

He stared at the candle, at the flame dancing in the undetectable current, at other candles whose flames had extinguished themselves.

Violette, God...

Nothing came to mind. Nothing but desperation. And fear.

Please, God...

He swallowed the emotions that threatened to surface, then quickly stood and left the chapel. It was all too much to pray about right now.

Violette

J am in the mall, hordes of
people shuffling past me and
through me with their bags and
boxes and looks of annoyance de-

December 1998

spite the theme of the holiday. Violette is sitting on a bench, staring unseeing at the crowd. It is the day before Christmas Eve, and
she still doesn't have anything for Saul.

Violette springs up from the seat and begins to wander. I know
her mind is grasping for possibilities. She is wondering what you
get for a guy you're madly in love with but have been dating for
only a few months. A guy who's not an artist—worse, who's a computer engineer. (I *still* don't get what it was he did every day.) I wish
I could direct her to a tie rack, but I know Violette; she is creative,
and a traditional gift would never make it on her list.

Alexine had suggested music, but I'd figured that was a dodgy
prospect, at least until you knew the person's collection backward

and forward and were sure not to get something he already had. Or would hate.

Xavier, being the fashion plate he was, had suggested clothes. He had commented to me how uncultured Saul's wardrobe could be, although he had to admit Saul had a few decent pieces and wore them well. Still, it was Xavier's opinion that the man needed a makeover, but I hadn't been sure if that was the message I wanted to send.

After ten minutes of aimless meandering, Violette sits on another bench to rack her brain. This is not going well. She is telling herself that she should have listened more over the last couple months and hidden away in her memory the passing comments he made about things he wanted or needed or loved. I wasn't good at that sort of thing, and my carelessness always came back to bite me when Christmas came around.

She feels like she *had* an idea somewhere, stuck in a storage box in her brain, but she just can't find it. I hope she doesn't come up with it. But of course she does, as I knew she would, and she almost laughs out loud with relief. She jumps from the bench and makes her way to the parking garage, plotting her next couple stops and singing "Jingle Bells" under her breath.

It is Christmas Eve, and I am with Violette and Saul at his apartment, which I had decorated for him one afternoon while he was at work. I'd been appalled that he didn't typically deck out the joint for the holidays; Alexine and I always dragged out the garland

and ornaments the day after Thanksgiving. Candles are burning and Sinatra is streaming from the stereo; they have just eaten a meal of spaghetti and salad—red and green making it the perfect Christmas dinner. The plan is to exchange gifts after they eat, and then go to a Christmas Eve service somewhere.

"Okay, you first," Saul insists as he hands her a small box. "You're a hard woman to shop for, you know that?"

"I am? How can that be? I hardly own anything!"

"Yeah, but…well, just trust me, you're hard to shop for." He shrugs. "Anyway, I figured with this I couldn't go wrong."

Violette rips away the wrapping to reveal a small flat rectangular box. I know her mind is racing in anticipation. *Flat: could be a watch, necklace, picture frame, albeit a very thin one.* She bites her lip and takes off the lid.

"I had no idea what you needed, so I thought this way you could get whatever you want." A gift certificate to some art supply chain store. I feel her dinner turn to lead in her stomach. He looks so proud of himself. Violette wants to smack him, and, honestly, so do I. It isn't even a store I usually went to because the prices were so high. I'd actually taken him once to my usual supplier; didn't he remember me raving about the place? What had he been thinking?

"Thanks!" Violette says as brightly as possible. Her disappointment doesn't show. "Great idea." I suppose that's accurate—if by "great" she means "lame idea that shows no creativity whatsoever." She's almost feeling guilty for how much better her gift is for him;

he is going to be so embarrassed. She hands him the box I had wrapped in paper I'd painted myself. "Merry Christmas."

"Wow, it's big. And heavy. My curiosity is definitely piqued." Violette beams as Saul eyes the package. "Did you make this paper?"

"Yep!"

He stares at the box. "But I don't want to rip it, then."

"It's wrapping paper. It's supposed to be ripped."

He frowns and begins to carefully pull the tape from the sides. "Oh sure. How would *that* look, me shredding your art."

"But I said you could!"

Nevertheless, he works at the tape until all the pieces come off and he can fold the paper up for later. I am secretly pleased at the care he has taken with it. He opens the white box inside and lifts out her gift.

"It's...um...wow," he stammers. "I take it you made this, too?"

"Well, I didn't *make* the box, but I decorated it, yes."

Saul slowly turns the wooden box over in his hands, inspecting the designs she'd painted and the metal shapes she'd adhered. "It's... well, wow! It's very... It's beautiful, babe, thanks." He quickly leans over to kiss her, then sets the box on his lap. "Is there a particular use you had in mind for it?"

"Well, of course you can use it for whatever you want, but I was thinking you could use it as a memory box, for all the little things you collect that need a place to live."

"Like...what kinds of little things?"

"Oh, you know—ticket stubs from the movies we go to, shells from the beach when we picnicked there, that sort of thing. Mine were taking up too much space, all piled on my dresser, so I figured you were probably having the same issue. And I know how you hate clutter, so I thought this would be a good solution." Violette smiles at him, reveling in the brilliance of her idea.

"Wow. So you save that sort of stuff, huh?"

She laughs. "Well, of course! Don't you?"

Saul scratches his neck, staring at the box. "Well, like you said, I hate clutter, so…"

"So…you *don't* save those things?"

"Not usually, no."

"What about the things I give you?"

"Your gifts? Of course I save those!"

"The sand dollar? The bookmark? The cards?"

"You gave me a bookmark?"

I can feel the steam gathering in my ears. "Yes, I did. The photo of the rocks under water?"

"That was the *end* of a photo you cropped."

"And when I gave it to you, I said, 'Here, it's a bookmark!' "

"No, you said, 'I was cropping photos and thought this still looked cool, *and it's just the right size for a bookmark.*' I didn't know you were expecting me to use it."

"Then why else would I give it to you?"

"I don't know. You're always giving me random junk like—"

"Junk?"

Saul curses under his breath. "I didn't mean junk, Violette, I swear; it just came out that way."

"So I suppose the cards and sand dollar were just junk too."

"Not junk! I just didn't think you expected me to hold on to them, that's all!"

"So you just throw them away?"

"Well…"

Violette huffs in disgust. "Well, no wonder you never give me anything; you don't have a sentimental bone in your body."

Saul's eyes bulge. "What are you talking about? I give you stuff all the time!"

"Like what?"

"Like I had the oil in your car changed for you, I gave you and Alexine those extra dishes so you'd have a matching set—"

Violette rolls her eyes. "Those aren't *gifts*. They're…they're practicalities! They're a disguised way of saying you don't trust someone to be able to take care of herself."

"That's ridiculous."

"No, it's true."

Saul glares for a moment, then throws his hands up in defeat. "Okay, you're right. I can't believe you've gotten this far living like you do, prioritizing your money the way you do, making the choices you do. Kudos to you for making it work for this long, but honestly, Violette, do you really think you can live an entire life that way?"

"I can't believe you're saying this."

"Well, believe it. I've done my best to go along with you and your whacked-out approach to life, but *come on!*"

I hear the blood singing in my ears. "I should have known," Violette says.

"Known what?"

"Known someone like you would be too rigid and too…too *afraid* to try stepping outside his comfort zone to consider a different way of living. You crawl off to your little crate of a cubicle every morning and crawl home to your little crate of an apartment every night, and every day is the same. You don't dream, you don't experiment, you don't let loose and do something silly because heaven forbid you lose control for five seconds! I can't live in a box, Saul. I can't confine myself to a daily grind that leaves no room for creativity the way you do. You may not agree with the way I live, but you said it yourself, it's worked for this long. And there's no reason why it can't keep working."

They stand on opposite sides of the room, staring at each other, the tone of their voices still rebounding off the walls, multiplying to fill the space with an almost tangible anger. Watching myself fight with the man I so desperately miss would have been intolerable, but I know what is coming next. I want to skip to that scene, but I don't have control.

Saul tosses the box onto the sofa and crosses his arms. "Well, if that's how you feel about me, I can't imagine you'd want to stick around, especially since you've been doing so well on your own. Why don't you go?"

Violette gapes at him, and I know she is desperately searching for words. When she doesn't move, he shakes his head in disgust and walks out of the room. A moment later the bedroom door slams.

I stand in the living room, suddenly cognizant of Sinatra still crooning on the stereo. My heart hurts so much it causes physical pain, and Violette wraps her arms around her stomach to keep everything from flying out the way it feels like it might. *What if this is it,* she worries. *What if it's over?* Her chin quivers, and she wants to take it all back—or at least bandage things up until they heal on their own.

For five minutes she stands in stunned silence, and I want to tell her what to say. Maybe she does hear me because, for the first time in her life, she knows exactly what to do, exactly what to say to make things right. As if on autopilot, she walks to the door of his bedroom and takes a deep breath. The words are already in position, queued up and waiting for her mouth to open so they can spill out and make everything right.

"I keep all my bank statements. They're in a shoe box, granted, but they're in chronological order. And I check all my credit card statements against my receipts every month. I actually found a fraudulent charge once, for a dating service I'd never even heard of.

"I thought it was the sweetest thing in the world that you took my car in for me. I never remember stuff like that. It's amazing I haven't run it into the ground yet. You probably saved me from a breakdown on the freeway.

"I think sometimes I assume you can read my mind, which is dumb, I know; I shouldn't expect you to know what I'm thinking or what I intend for things to mean. You're totally right, I never said, 'Here, I made this bookmark for you.' I just assumed that you'd realize what I meant. Sometimes I feel silly giving you things because I don't want to be the gushy girlfriend, but at the same time I want to shower you with gifts and affection because I love you so much. So I end up doing things but not explaining why."

I am proud of Violette. She takes a deep breath and keeps going.

"So, how about if I stop expecting you to be clairvoyant, and I'll let you teach me how to, say, create a budget? Maybe I could actually afford to get a new car if I was being a little more responsible with my money. And we could maybe paint your apartment, redecorate a little—only if you wanted to, of course. Because really it's fine the way it is now. But it might be fun, you know? And I'll totally let you boss me around when we paint; you can sit and eat grapes and I'll do all the work. But only if you want to, of course."

The door opens slowly, and I feel my heart swell. "What if I pick all neutrals?"

"Neutrals are great! Neutrals provide the perfect backdrop for art. And heaven knows you have access to some of the best art available. You might even be able to get a custom piece."

"I'm so sorry, Violette."

"I am too."

"Do you forgive me?"

"Only if you forgive me first."

"I completely forgive you."

"And *I* completely forgive *you*."

The feel of Saul's arms around my waist makes me nearly collapse. I can hardly stand it when he suddenly breaks off the extended kissing to say, "The Christmas Eve service!"

"Oh no! Can we still make it?"

He studies his watch. "If we leave now and speed a little, I think we'll be fine."

"Which one are we going to?" Violette asks.

"I thought we agreed on the Presbyterian church?"

"I didn't think we'd agreed on anything yet. What about the Unitarian church Xavier told me about?"

"Unitarians don't even believe Jesus was divine; what's the point of Christmas if you don't believe he was the Christ?"

"I don't know if I believe that anyway."

"You don't?"

Violette holds up a hand. "Halt. I can see where this is going, and it's not toward the door and the car and a Christmas Eve service. Let's go to the Presbyterian church, and then next year I can choose."

Saul smirks. "Next year? Planning awfully far ahead, aren't you?"

Violette bats her eyes. "Just thinking positively, my dear." She plants one more kiss on his cheek before taking his hand to lead him to the door. A profound sense of relief floods my system, now that I am past that ugly event and on to happier memories.

Memories? Is that what this is? What's going on?

I have no time to figure it out. I am in the car, watching Violette hum along to the radio, her hand in Saul's.

*C*hristian was home.

Alexine and Xavier had finally convinced him to go back to his own bed for a night, to get a decent meal and a shower and some rest. Leaving the hospital was surreal; he hadn't seen the outside world since coming in with Violette two days ago. It felt like a month. He stared at the dashboard of his car for five minutes, wondering why it looked so unfamiliar. He took a wrong turn going home, and the neighborhood he found himself in was like a foreign country. When he finally made it home, he sat on the couch, staring at the wall, wondering why he'd never thought to buy one of Violette's paintings for his empty walls.

He didn't know what to do with himself. He had a mental list of things he knew he should do, but no motivation to move from the sofa. His body was leaden. The television was too loud. He wanted to eat but nothing sounded good. Eventually he fell asleep to escape the clamoring of his stomach and the to-do list rattling around his head, only to wake up an hour later to more of the same.

He managed to lift the television remote; the effort was akin to lifting a barbell. He found a new show but couldn't follow the plot and fell asleep again. The screen was snowy when he awoke the second time, and the clock on the mantel said 3:12. *This is nuts,* he thought. He'd only planned on being home one night, but at his rate of progress, he'd be here until the next evening just trying to get things done. He finally forced himself from the sofa and staggered into the kitchen to throw together as much of a meal as he could. While soup warmed on the stove, he ran down to the mailbox and brought up what little mail he'd received in the last couple days. Then, in between spoonfuls of minestrone, he compiled a list of tasks that absolutely could not be ignored.

The burst of productivity pleased him and fueled him for the next couple hours. By the time the sun was rising he'd crossed out most of his list. Only a few items remained before he could justify returning to the hospital. He was in his bedroom pulling clean clothes from his dresser when the photo from his wedding caught his eye. Cynthia beamed, even in black and white, and his lovesick eyes stared into hers as if she were his salvation.

The photo arrested his actions; he sank onto the bed without removing his eyes from her face. He saw himself in the weeks leading up to her death, saw himself resigned to his impending loss, remembered the conversations that flipped between what was for dinner and what songs Cynthia wanted at her funeral. He saw himself leave her grave—his parents and hers on either side—politely turning down the offered meals and company, saw himself sitting at home reviewing case files with the television on to break the silence, saw himself edging further into the middle of the bed and eventually taking the whole space over. He saw himself slipping his Bible into a drawer one day, justifying yet another week of staying home from church.

He'd never stared vacantly at the television. He'd never found himself trying to compose a to-do list at three in the morning over a bowl of minestrone because he'd lost two days in mental deep freeze. He'd never pleaded with God in a stained-glass chapel. He'd never acted with Cynthia the way he was acting with Violette. What was wrong with him?

The prayer he'd attempted in the chapel returned to him, and his hands started shaking. *Oh, God.* Hope. The difference was hope. *Oh God, please.* Cynthia had none. The doctors made that clear from the beginning. Sometimes you are simply powerless. Even God's hands seemed tied; a miracle of that magnitude would be like watching a shattered window piece itself back together right in front of your eyes. But this time no rock-solid diagnosis left him inevitably doomed—he had no firm pronouncements from blunt doctors who dropped their bombs and left him to grieve alone. This time he had more question marks than periods, more maybe's than never's. And knowing that possibilities existed meant he couldn't resign himself to anything. He couldn't close doors in his mind and soul and move his life ahead over the speed bump of the Tragedy He Couldn't Change. He was stalled at Violette's bedside, waiting. Hoping.

He recognized that he had tremendous fear of the unpredictable, and this situation caused him so much panic and terror that he thought he'd detonate. He was doing his best to stuff his emotions, to ignore his fear, to reason his way through everything, but he wasn't successful. He also knew his anger toward God for not doing more for Cynthia was still lingering. But sheer desperation was beginning to eclipse his anger. He just didn't see himself getting over this the way he had before, and he was ready to try it out with God again.

Christian felt his soul crack. Perhaps that's what God had to do, just the way doctors sometimes have to refracture a bone in order to set it correctly. No words were spoken—no sounds made at all—as the anger and hurt and frustration poured forth. But he felt light enter his shadowed corners as he surrendered. His hands steadied, and he lay down on the bed, overcome with a new exhaustion. But this time he didn't fight the sleep, and he didn't feel guilty about being away from Violette.

When he awoke, the room was awash in sunshine, and his heart felt buoyed. He had taken hold of hope.

Violette

"Picnic basket?"

"Check."

"Food and wine in basket?"

"Check."

"Nerve?"

Violette sighs. "Check, I think."

I smile. I'll be her nerve.

"You're really going to do this?" Alexine asks.

"Yes, I am."

Alexine folds her hands beneath her chin, striking a matronly pose. "I can't believe our little girl's gonna get engaged!"

"Well, that depends on what the guy says."

"Oh, come on; you honestly think he'd say no?"

Violette flops onto the couch. "No, I guess not. I just worry he'll be turned off by my making the move."

Alexine joins her and pats her knee. "He's grown quite a bit in the last year. I think he might appreciate it."

"Really?"

"Well, let's hope so for your sake."

The doorbell rings and both their eyes bulge. "This is it!" Alexine squeals. Violette jumps up and smoothes her sundress before opening the door.

"Hey, gorgeous."

"Hey yourself." She falls against him and meets his kiss with one of her own. I feel the tingle on my lips. "All set?"

"I am, but these flowers may need a drink first." From behind his back he brings forth a bouquet of gerber daisies. "Happy anniversary, babe."

Violette claps with delight. "They're beautiful! Oh, thank you, Saul." She kisses him again, then takes the flowers. "Come in and let me put them in a vase." She turns to Alexine and makes an "Isn't he a darling?" face. "Look, Lex, I got flowers!"

Alexine smiles. "Good choice, Mr. Corterm."

Violette skips to the kitchen and fills a vase with water. She's reviewing her plan; I'm reviewing the past. She arranges the flowers in the vase, then brings them to the living room and places them on the coffee table. "Perfect. Thank you, love." She kisses him again, then picks up the basket. "Ready?"

"Ready."

She follows him out the door, aiming one last knowing grin at Alexine before heading for the stairs. My stomach twitches and dances the twist; the plan has been set in motion, and she can't back out now. Alexine is already on the phone, calling X to let him know they are on their way.

"Oh, I forgot to ask you," she says. I'm impressed by how casual she sounds. "Can we stop by the gallery before we go to the beach?"

"No problem. What's up?"

"X needs me to sign a contract for a new piece. I forgot to do it earlier today, and he needs it for tomorrow morning." The lie sounds thin. Why hadn't I thought of something more convincing?

But apparently he falls for it, because he says nothing more; he just opens the car door for her and packs the picnic basket in the trunk.

The ride to the gallery feels faster than usual, and I know Violette is wondering whether Xavier has enough time to get all the candles lit. Her mind is racing, going over all the details and looking for the one thing she is sure she has forgotten. In no time they are pulling up in the alley behind the gallery and parking at the door. "Should I just wait here?" Saul asks.

I watch Violette's expression and decide that I should have been an actress. "Ah, why don't you come in? And bring the basket, if you don't mind—I don't want the cheese to melt in the trunk."

Saul sends her a look she can't decipher, but says nothing and does as she asked. She leads the way into the gallery's office area where Xavier is straightening out a stack of papers on the desk. "Hey, you two lovebirds! Happy anniversary." Xavier smiles and Violette searches his face for any clue that he hadn't gotten everything done. He simply smiles apologetically at Saul. "Sorry she had to drag you here for business first." He glances at the basket in Saul's hand. "That your new man purse or something?"

Saul chuckles. "Violette feared for the constitution of the cheese."

"Ah, I see." He takes a paper off the top of the stack and hands it to Violette. "I'm on my way out, so just leave this on the desk when you're done reading and signing. Oh, and could you lock the front door too? I'm running late."

"No problem," Violette says. "Saul, why don't you go lock the door, and I'll get this thing signed?"

Saul shrugs and sets down the basket. "Sure. Have a good night, Xavier."

Saul leaves the office. Xavier beams and gives her a quick hug before wordlessly heading out the door. She quickly hits "play" on the stereo and grabs the basket, takes a deep breath, and heads into the gallery.

She finds Saul standing in the gallery, hands in his pockets, staring at the blanket ringed by votive candles. The music starts and he glances up in surprise, then sees her as she enters. A slow smile spreads across his face. "Had to sign a contract, huh?"

Violette bats her eyes and saunters closer. "Maybe just a teensy little lie. I hope you're not offended."

"I think I can forgive you."

Violette sets the basket down and wraps her arms around his neck. "Happy anniversary, darling."

His kisses return the sentiment, and I feel alive again. But after a moment he pulls back. "So what's really in that basket?"

She laughs. "Food! We're still picnicking; hence the blanket." She pulls him down to the quilt and drags the basket over. "You pour the wine and I'll fill your plate." She hands him two wine glasses and a bottle, then sets to work preparing cheese, crackers, and fruit on a plastic plate. "We even have three courses, so I hope you're hungry."

"You have three courses in that small basket? I'm impressed."

"Well..." She smirks. "Yes and no. You'll see."

She hands him his plate and makes one of her own, then closes the basket and takes her glass of wine and holds it aloft. "Cheers to us."

"Cheers to us." He taps his glass to hers, then kisses her before sipping the wine. I feel a fleeting sensation of warmth in my chest. "This is quite the production, babe. Well done."

She beams. "Thank you. I'm glad you noticed. It took quite a bit of planning, and you know how I am with planning."

"Even more reason for me to be impressed."

"You've got that right." She winks and pops a grape in her

mouth, though I know she's lost her appetite. Her face looks calm, but her inner nervousness is causing my stomach to feel squeamish.

Time disappears, and dessert is ready to be served. Violette reaches into the basket, her hand shaking. She doesn't know how her surprise will be received or what surprise is in store for her. I have no desire to warn her, even if I could. "Dessert has two parts," she says, and I hear the tremor in her voice. She pulls out a medium-sized box and hands it to him. "Open."

Saul grins and pulls off the lid, revealing a chocolate frosted cake with *I love you* written in red script. "This looks good," he says, wagging his eyebrows.

"Well, before we cut it…" Violette gulps and takes the box from him. Laying it aside, she sits up on her knees and takes his hand. "Saul, I love you."

A shadow crosses his face. "I love you too," he says slowly.

I feel my stomach lurch as Violette panics. That wasn't the look she'd hoped for. She charges ahead before she can change her mind. "This has been the— I mean, this *year* has been the best year my life— I mean *of* my life." She swallows, cursing her brain that is moving too fast for her mouth. I try to slow her down by touching her shoulder, but she continues on. "I haven't loved anyone as much as I've loved you." She reaches for his hand and knocks over his wine glass. She bites her lip and grabs a napkin. "I can't believe this," she mutters. "I'm so sorry."

Saul helps her blot away the spilled wine, then takes the napkin from her hand and entwines her fingers in his. "Violette," he says, a smile spreading slowly on his face. "Is this what I think it is?"

Tears of frustration prick my eyes as Violette stresses about her upset plans. "I don't know. What do you think it is, besides me botching one of the biggest moments of my life?"

"It's *you* botching the biggest moment of *my* life."

Violette's eyes grow wide, and as I feel blood rushing to my face, I want to assure her that things aren't as bad as she thinks they are. "I *ruined* it? How? Unless you don't..." She can't bring herself to express her fear.

Saul stands up and pulls her to her feet. After a kiss that makes my brain buzz, he releases one of her hands and sighs. "Yes, you ruined my evening because you nearly beat me to the punch." He kneels down and brings a ring from his pocket. "I'll accept your proposal if you accept mine."

Violette stares at the white gold band and the diamond that sparkles in the sunset light streaming in through the windows. "Oh my."

"Hope I didn't ruin your evening too."

Violette laughs and sinks down to the blanket beside him. "Not at all!" They share a kiss that leaves my whole body tingling and aching for more.

When they finally part, Violette sighs. "But from now on I'm leaving the planning to you. It's so much more stressful than spontaneity."

*C*hristian could have pre-
dicted, though it wasn't what
he'd hoped for, that no change in
Violette's condition occurred during

the time he'd been home. He was back at the hospital, back in the
now-familiar environment of beeping machines and brisk nurses
and general silence punctuated by voices in the hall or the occasional visitor. No one was any wiser about what was happening in
Violette's brain, but Christian was no longer as anxious. He believed he and God had come to an understanding last night, and
part of the deal was that Violette would live. Nobody offered a
guarantee on the long-term effects she might suffer, but Christian
knew he could deal with it—and Violette would too, with his help.

He had the journal out again. He was getting used to writing in
it; now he understood firsthand why it was such a standard suggestion by therapists of all stripes. He wished he'd tried it earlier, like

when Cynthia died, because he had a feeling he could have saved himself a few years of pain. Regardless, he was going to take advantage of it now and be much improved when Violette woke up.

"When Violette woke up" was his current subject. What would happen then? He had no doubt in his mind that he loved her, but he did doubt just how much the sentiment was returned. He knew Violette *liked* him, and her kisses proved she was attracted to him, but did she really *love* him? *This* was what bothered him. He really couldn't tell.

Their dating relationship hadn't started quite the way he'd hoped. After that first dinner date he'd been convinced of a mutual attraction. All he needed was one more good date and the guts to end it with a kiss on the cheek—or mouth if he thought the night had gone *really* well. He'd been so proud of himself for being ready to pursue a relationship that he hadn't considered that Violette might not be there yet. And the way she'd hugged him after dinner that first night, her arms lingering around his neck a few seconds more than really necessary, sure made it seem like she was ready.

He'd put a lot of thought into their next meeting. He wanted to take her somewhere nice, but not too nice—someplace quiet so they could talk, but not so intimate as to make her uncomfortable. He considered eight different restaurants before choosing The Wharf. Then nerves kicked in, and he waited four days longer than he'd planned to call her. He tried not to dwell on the fact that she hadn't called him during that time, either. He reminded himself that she had said "Call me," not "I'll call you," and that just because someone is willing to have you call them doesn't mean they're comfortable calling you. The fact that she'd asked him to call her *had* to bode well for him, right?

A week after their dinner, he finally got up his nerve. After psyching himself up over lunch, he dialed her number—and then found himself praying for her answering machine. No such luck. She answered on the third ring, and as far as he could tell, she sounded happy to hear from him. He chatted inanely for a few minutes before taking the plunge. "If you're not busy Friday, I'd love to take you out to dinner." *Love?* He kicked himself for the choice of words. That sounded way too eager. But her reaction gave him more cause for concern.

"Oh." It was the kind of "Oh" that is short for "Oh boy, I didn't see this coming," followed by a pause that sounds like someone racking her brain for an excuse. "Dinner? Um…yeah, sure. That sounds fine." That sounds *fine?* Hardly the response he'd been expecting.

"If you're not up for it…," he offered, trying to let her off the hook if she was really dreading it. The last thing he wanted was a dinner partner who felt like a prisoner.

"No, no, I'd love to go. Honestly. What time would you like to pick me up?"

Pick her up! Now *that* was a good sign. If she really wasn't looking forward to it, the last thing she'd want was to be picked up and trapped with him for both the ride there and the ride back. Maybe she had just been taken off guard. He thought he'd made it fairly clear at dinner the week before that he was interested, but maybe he'd been too subtle. She just hadn't been expecting this new invitation, that's all.

By the time they settled on a time and said their good-byes, Christian felt like he'd run a marathon. His mind shuffled up the memory of junior high homeroom and the note Katie Carlisle had dropped onto his desk on her way to the pencil sharpener: "Do you like me? Circle Yes or No." How much easier this whole thing would be if he could just be that forward. Heck, it had worked for him and Katie. They'd dated for four whole weeks, which was long enough for him to have his first slow dance and kiss on the cheek. But no, being an adult meant all this finessing and planning and energy. Why was that? Why couldn't he just come out and say what he was thinking? He decided to give that line of action some thought before Friday.

He arrived eight minutes late, feeling tremendously guilty for it. Traffic had thwarted his punctuality, and the cell phone he forgot to charge because he used it so infrequently gave its last dying beep as he tried to call Violette to let her know. As he made his way up the walk to her front door, Violette's face appeared in the window, and seconds later the door was opened before he was anywhere near it. "I'm so sorry," he said. "The traffic—"

"Oh, no, not a problem. Don't worry." But the look on her face told him that she hadn't been casually waiting.

"I would have called too, but my phone was dead. I always forget to charge it."

"Really, it's no big deal."

"Are you sure? Because you look a little…I'm not sure."

A blush crept into her cheeks and he almost felt contrite, except it made her that much prettier. She waved her hand, embarrassed. "Oh, my overactive imagination had you in all sorts of tragic circumstances, that's all. Don't mind me."

She'd been worried about him! Well, that had to mean something. He smiled in what he hoped was a reassuring way. "My imagination tends to do the same thing. Anyway, are you ready?"

"Sure am. So where are we going?"

"The Wharf. Have you been there?" Her expression and pause gave her answer. "Oh," he said slowly. "I'm guessing that was a place you and Saul went."

"Just a few times, yes. But really, that's okay." She smiled. "I can't very well avoid some of the best seafood in the state for the rest of my life, can I?"

"We don't have to—"

"No, Christian, really, it's all right." She squeezed his arm. "It'll be good for me, you know? I haven't been there since…well, in a long time. And now I'm craving lobster, so we don't have a choice."

Her countenance did seem genuinely okay, and he wasn't going to contradict her. "The Wharf it is, then! You might want to grab a jacket. It's chilly out here tonight." As she retreated back into the house to get her things, Christian's mind flew through some quick calculations. If he had things right, then her concern for his well-being minus his choice of restaurants plus her hand on his arm equaled a chance. He was still safe.

Violette seemed intent on assuring him she really was okay; for the entire ride she kept up the conversation and was livelier than he'd ever seen her. It wasn't until they were walking up to the giant carved wood doors that her façade faltered. "First date," she finally said. "And two anniversaries." She gave him a pathetic smile. "Don't you just hate memories sometimes? Like when they come back to haunt a perfectly good evening?"

"Mario's Spaghetti House, every Tuesday night for three years," Christian said. "And where does my mother want to go before flying home after the funeral?

"You're kidding."

"Nope."

"That's just cruel!"

"Well, she always was the forgetful type; chances are she didn't remember a single time Cynthia and I had mentioned it."

Violette laughed, and the light in her eyes told Christian the equation was still balanced in his favor. "Talk about bucking up and getting on with your life."

He shrugged. "Had to happen eventually; two days after her burial was just a little sooner than I'd anticipated."

Violette winced in sympathy and then led him into the restaurant, further convincing him that she was going to be okay with this.

The evening went as well as he could have hoped, and by the end he was confident that the timing and mood were right for a frank confession of his feelings. Over their final glass of wine before taking the check, Christian waited for an opening, then pounced when the conversation lulled.

"Violette, I wanted to let you know something," he began. She cocked her head expectantly, absently swirling the wine in her glass. "I've really enjoyed the time we've spent together recently. I didn't think I was ready to date anyone, but you've proved me wrong. Now, I know you said before that you weren't sure you were ready for this. I want you to know that I'm fine taking it at whatever pace you want, and, um…" He ran out of words. "I guess that's it." He smiled sheepishly and gulped down some water to avoid looking her in the eyes while she considered his offer.

"Wow. That was the most straightforward declaration I've ever heard." She let out a laugh—a time-buying laugh—and Christian could see in her face that he'd made a terrible mistake.

"You're not interested at all," he stated, unable to keep the disappointment out of his voice.

Violette's face fell. She covered her face with her hands, then reached out and took his hands in hers. "Christian, you're an incredible man. The first *man* I think I've ever been friends with, really. Saul was a…a guy, you know? Anyway, that's irrelevant…" She sighed and closed her eyes a moment. "What I'm trying to say is that I really value our friendship, but I'm not where you are yet. I thought about it this week, because of what you'd said before, and I was ready to *pretend* for a while to see if it worked; but I think you'd agree that's probably not the healthiest thing to do. It has nothing to do with you, though, okay? I'm just not ready to replace Saul."

Christian nodded, digesting her words. "You're pretty good at the whole straightforward declaration thing too, you know that?" He smiled and winked, trying to show her no harm done, despite the fact that he felt like a colossal fool.

She sat back and ran her hands through her hair. "I've really botched things up, haven't I?"

"No, Violette, not at all. I understand where you're coming from, believe me."

"If you were my therapist, would you think I was making the right decision?"

He laughed. "If I were your therapist, we'd have a serious conflict of interest."

She gave him a half smile and kicked him gently under the table. "Come on, for real: good decision or not, in your professional opinion?"

Christian settled back in his seat and studied her, trying to be objective. "In my professional opinion…good decision, with one caveat. If you think in terms of replacing Saul, you'll never be able to move on; you loved him and of course would never want someone to take his place. But when you come to the place where you realize you can love someone else—not *instead* of Saul but *along with* Saul, just like you can love both Alexine and Xavier as your friends at the same time—then you'll be in a very good place."

A small smile tugged at the corners of Violette's mouth. "And when I get there, maybe we can go out to dinner to celebrate?"

He could tell she felt bad for turning him down. This was her offering of hope for him. How could he not be crazy about someone who was trying to be so careful with him? He smiled back, hoping his face conveyed his understanding. "Only if you let me treat."

I couldn't believe it when she came around. But despite what she claims, I can tell she's holding back. A part of her is not yet fully engaged. I don't want to push too hard; but at the same time, if she's not at the same place I am, then where does that leave us? If she's working on it, that's one thing; but if not, then there would be no chance of us ever

Christian stared at the journal. No chance of them ever what? Marrying? Now *that* was a possibility he'd never truly allowed himself to consider. Sure, the concept had hovered at the outer edges of his mind, but he'd not yet let the thought really take shape. After these last few days, though, he knew clearly what his feelings were for Violette, and marriage was definitely the next step for them in his eyes. But only if she was ready.

Would she ever be?

Violette

November 1999

o what's all this hype about weddings being so great?"

Alexine raises an eyebrow at Violette and sits back on her painting stool. "I take it things aren't coming together like you'd hoped?"

Violette tosses her backpack into a corner and pulls on an apron. "I hadn't 'hoped' anything, really. I wasn't one of those girls planning my wedding from the time I was eight. So I'm flexible, you know? I'm not trying to force my life-long dream of a wedding on him or anything; but I swear, you'd think I was asking for the moon!" She ties a bandanna over her hair and begins pulling acrylic tubes from the cabinet, throwing four of them onto the floor before slamming the cabinet door. "All I asked for—honestly, this is it, this is all I really care about—is having Pastor Drew do the ceremony and that we do it on the beach. That is *all*. Is that so demanding?"

"Well, what's Saul's complaint?"

"That I'm not actually a member of Church in the Canyon, so why have them do it when his family's pastor has married everyone since forever."

Alexine considers this as she dabs at her canvas. "Well, I can see how Saul might want to fall back on family tradition."

I feel heat rising to my face as Violette glares at her.

"I didn't say I agreed with him," Alexine corrects. "Just that I understood him. Easy there, kitty."

Violette sighs and swishes a paintbrush in a water jar. "What's ridiculous is that he hasn't even *been* to this church of his since he was in high school. I go to Church in the Canyon almost every week now, and I swear the only reason he started going back to his church is because he wanted to spite me."

"What?"

Violette rolls her eyes. "He thinks CitC is flaky. The candles and stuff freak him out; way too experiential for him. He's more comfortable in an oak pew singing songs written in Old English."

"Have you gone to his church with him? To show him that you're willing to compromise a bit, or at least try to see things from his point of view?"

Violette bends her head to her canvas and begins to paint, pointedly ignoring Alexine's remark. I wish I could tell Violette that someday she'd wish she could go to his church with him every day if it meant seeing him again.

"Violette?" Alexine asks, noticing the sudden quiet.

Violette huffs. "Oh sure, Lex, like I'm going to fit in there. Please."

"You're just as bad as he is."

"No, I'm not!"

Alexine arches her brows and Violette pouts. "Alexine, seriously, I'd never even set foot in a church until CitC had that community art show. You've been there—you've seen how unchurchy it is. I can guarantee you Saul's little stone chapel with its pews and hymns would spit me out like a bite of rotten apple."

"Oh, come on, Violette."

Violette ignores her, slapping some paint on the canvas and cursing under her breath.

Alexine continues, and I want to cheer her on. "You may go every week to CitC, but it's not like you're *that* into it, right? I mean, it's not like you've converted or anything. So maybe you should let Saul's guy do the ceremony since he actually believes their stuff. *Does* he believe their stuff?"

Violette mixes two colors on the palette. "I think so, yeah."

"Is that okay with you?"

She groans and rubs her forehead. "I don't know, honestly. I mean, I feel judgmental if I say no, and if I say yes, my answer doesn't sit right with me."

"Have you guys talked about religion at all?"

Violette dabs her canvas. "Not exactly. We keep inviting each other to church and keep turning each other down. Nothing has really changed with him since he started going, so I guess that's good—no bait and switch, you know?"

"What do you mean?"

Violette sits back and examines the paint she's laid down. "I mean he didn't get all preachy on me and all self-righteous and holier-than-thou when he started going back."

"Well, so, doesn't that say that maybe his church isn't so bad?"

"Maybe," comes her grudging answer after a considerable pause.

Alexine smiles. "*You* didn't get all preachy and self-righteous and holier-than-thou when you started going to CitC, so isn't it in the realm of possibility that his church isn't as bad as you're making it out to be?"

"Well, maybe—but I don't really go in for all that stuff, so of course I didn't act that way."

Alexine settles back on her stool and crosses her arms. "Which leads us to the next inevitable question: Why do you keep going if you don't even believe what they teach?"

Violette plops her brush into a water jar. "Because...I don't know. The people are really nice. The atmosphere is inviting. Their band is great, although the lyrics are a little weird. It's a different social scene, that's all."

"Don't you get tired of hearing all the religious stuff though?"

"Not really. It's interesting." She shrugs. "I mean, yeah, some of it is just plain bizarre, but a lot of the principles are good. You know, love your neighbor, do unto others, do not kill…who wouldn't agree with that?"

Alexine chuckles. "Not many people. But I believe that without church, thank you very much."

Violette throws her a look, and I wonder why I hadn't talked religion with her more often. "You should come some time, if for no other reason than to see the hottie guitarist."

Alexine's smile widens. "There's a hottie guitarist?"

"*And* a hottie drummer. And the pastor's not so bad, either, although I think he might already be married. But it makes the sermons easier to listen to when they're coming from him, you know?"

Alexine laughs and waves her hand to dismiss the topic. "Look, I'll think about it, okay? But we still haven't solved your ceremony problem."

Violette swivels back to the canvas with a growl. "I *suppose* I could check out his church—*just once*—in the name of solidarity. I mean, he *is* going to be my husband, right? So I guess I should try to be at least a little supportive. But I don't plan to change my mind on the ceremony thing."

The scene shifts, and Violette is sitting in Saul's car, arms crossed as she stares out the window. I look over at Saul from my place in the backseat and see brooding on his face. He's annoyed with her.

"It's just that it's a big step for me, Saul," Violette attempts. "I'm comfortable at CitC, and I don't think I'm going to be comfortable at your church, that's all."

The situation comes flooding to mind, and I don't blame Saul for being upset. I *had* promised to go to his church, so it really hadn't been fair of me to get all weird about it at the last second. "You're always pushing me to try news things," he says, "but the second I turn the tables, you freak out."

She opens her mouth to argue, but realizes he's right. "I hadn't thought of it that way before."

"You think *I'm* comfortable with some of the stuff you ask me to do? No way! But I do it because I know it makes you happy to go to karaoke bars or to plays with audience participation…"

I watch Violette's body slump slowly, and I know she's disappointed with herself. She searches for a rebuttal and stammers through some half-baked sentences that eventually fizzle out into sighs of frustration. I lean over to whisper words of wisdom into Violette's ear, to give her a clue as to which tack to take so their conversation won't derail. But before I can act, I am Violette again, retorting with words I don't want to say. "This is *so* different, though, Saul. Traditional church people are a completely different species."

"*I'm* traditional church people, Violette."

"No, you're not. You might have been, once, but it's not like you changed back when you started going to church again."

He looked at her. "I haven't?"

"No, thank goodness."

"It would be that awful if I did?"

"Well, it would obviously depend on how you changed, but I doubt it would be for the better; so yes, it would be awful. I wouldn't be able to marry some religious freak."

"So religious people are all freaks."

"Most, yes."

"But of course not your precious CitC tribe."

"No, actually, some of them are, which is why I haven't bought into the whole scam. But *their* first priority is loving people, and from what I've experienced of traditional Christianity, its first priority is labeling people and sticking them in boxes so they can sit in judgment over them."

"So where did this 'experience' come from?"

"The family across the street who wouldn't let me play with their daughter because I was a 'bad influence,' a conclusion they came to only because I slipped up and swore when I stubbed my toe in their living room. The two girls I got stuck with on a history project in junior high science who said I was a heathen and going to hell because I didn't go to church. The idiots who call people like Xavier names I can't even bring myself to repeat." That shut him up, but I'm not sure what I won in that conversation.

Now I am sitting in a wooden pew. Saul sits to the left of Violette, and on the other side is an unruly three-year-old whose mother tries unsuccessfully to distract him with crayons. The boy becomes enamored with Violette's fuzzy sweater and pets her as if she were a dog, occasionally pulling on a thread to see what happens.

Saul looks at her expectantly, and she graciously responds with a nod to admit that it isn't awful. Then the congregation sings a song she knows from CitC, and Violette belts out the women's part as though she really believes the words—I have to laugh at the shock on Saul's face. The congregation is a lot more mixed in terms of age than CitC, where the oldest person she'd seen couldn't have been more than forty. Here the range is more like infant to eighty, and the mix of musical styles reflects that diversity. During the children's message, all the little kids flock to the front to sit at the pastor's knee and listen to a Bible story. Then most of them run off to children's church, save for the sweater-unraveling preschooler and a few others whose voices can occasionally be heard begging for a cracker or juice. The pastor is delivering his message now, and unlike at CitC, everyone's Bible is open and he is talking almost exclusively about the text. I know Violette is waiting for the three main points, but they won't come.

Now people are streaming to the front of the church to receive communion. I watch Violette's face, knowing this is one of those parts of the whole Christianity thing that used to freak me out. "Whose bright idea was it to take such innocent ingredients as wine and bread and turn them into symbols of a dead man's flesh and blood?" I would say to Alexine. "How much more revolting could it be?" Ever since I heard communion explained at CitC for the first time, I'd had a hard time with grapes and toast in any form.

Violette watches Saul join the throng that moves down the center aisle. I can feel her fingers rubbing her arms for comfort as she absorbs the truth that Saul really does believe all this stuff. The tortuous death of an innocent man, the claim that he'd come back to life, angels and devils, God. She's handling it well, despite the fact that she considers it all a jumble of fantastic stories and fantasy with some good moral teaching thrown in. We watch Saul walk toward us, and Violette smiles. She can't deny that in all other ways he is perfectly normal, and that gives her a little hope.

After people shuffle back to their seats, they sing one more song. Music continues to play, but people begin picking up coats and bulletins and Bibles, making their way toward the doors. Saul wordlessly takes Violette's hand and leads her out into the foyer, through the masses, to the front doors that let them out to the parking lot. Once they are free of the crowd, he kisses her cheek. "So?"

"It was…interesting."

"As stressful an experience as you'd been expecting?"

"No, I suppose not."

To his credit, he doesn't say *I told you so;* instead he kisses her once more. "I'm glad you came. I won't bug you about it again, so if you ever want to come, just let me know, okay?"

She kisses him back. "Okay." Then she stops. "What did we do for Christmas Eve last year?"

Saul frowns in thought. "Um...we went...we went to that church on the corner of Main and Tenth, remember? Because we fought and were late for the service here."

"Ah, that's right...well...if I remember correctly, the deal was that I could choose where to go this year."

Saul sighs and gives her a resigned smile. "Guess I'll be experiencing CitC next month, eh?"

Violette takes his hand. "Well, at least it's Christmas, so the candles won't seem nearly as weird."

C hristian was running late, but he couldn't get himself to move from the couch. He'd made the mistake of letting nostalgia get

the best of him, and now he was glued to the television, aching with the weight of the memories that pressed down on his shoulders.

Today would have been their fifteenth wedding anniversary. For the first time the date had snuck up on him; usually the square on his calendar practically glowed. He knew it was a healthy sign that he hadn't obsessed about it as he had the past couple years, but on the other hand, he didn't like the fact that he'd nearly forgotten about it. To make up for the near lapse, he had put in their wedding video to watch while he ate his breakfast, and now the cereal bowl was long empty and the video was coming to an end.

He also wasn't too pleased with the number of details he'd forgotten about the wedding. The bird trapped in the rafters of the church that chirped nonstop through the sermon, then fell silent when they exchanged their vows. The bridesmaid—one of twelve—who tripped on her dress and nearly brought down the groomsman who was her escort. The terse handshake from Cynthia's father and minimal embrace from her mother just before they left on their honeymoon. Nearly every scene of the video included something his memory had long ago purged, and he lost track of the number of times he thought, *I'd forgotten about that.*

Watching himself with Cynthia was surreal. They both looked so young—a trait Cynthia's genes allowed her to hold onto over the years while Christian's age had always shown plainly on his face. He looked ridiculous in the tuxedo, being too gangly and inexperienced to know how to carry himself; but Cynthia, the debutante, the sorority girl, looked like she'd been born to model wedding dresses. Her southern grace and charm were evident, as was his middle-class, midwestern practicality. Bless her soul, she'd tried so hard to cultivate him, but they both knew it was a losing battle; and while she never really minded, it was for her parents' sake she'd tried at all. He'd almost made the cut: Ivy League education, fraternity president, Protestant upbringing. He'd even gained a couple bonus points for the fencing trophy and graduating valedictorian from Yale's School of Psychology—granted, the psychology part of the degree was one of the things Cynthia's parents frowned upon. It wasn't *real* medicine, after all. Oh, and the Michigan upbringing. Apparently it was hardly possible to be properly raised north of Tennessee. He never really understood the issue, which Cynthia tried her best to downplay.

They'd met Christian's junior year. His fraternity, Alpha Zeta Nu, hosted the Kappa Delta Pi sorority for a Thanksgiving dinner dance, and he'd been seated next to sophomore Cynthia Truman. She had the most beautiful hair Christian had ever seen, although he had to admit he hadn't often noticed anyone's hair, so he didn't have a lot to compare it to. Her accent turned his knees to butter, yet he still asked her to dance; and despite how little he actually knew about formal dancing and how weak with infatuation his legs were, he managed not to step on her feet or appear too klutzy. He also managed to get a whiff of that beautiful hair. It smelled like coconut.

As a house officer—he'd been treasurer that year—he'd had a lot of responsibilities that evening, so after their one dance he found himself being pulled into duty and saying good-bye to Cynthia. Two days later he had her phone number and was calling for a date, and by the end of that school year they were talking engagement.

They waited to marry until Cynthia graduated. Christian was immersed in his graduate studies, and she went to work teaching humanities at an all-girls prep school near Yale. He brought in almost half their income working as a grad assistant for two professors on top of his own school load, but Cynthia's parents were appalled that she was shouldering the bulk of their financial responsibilities. This only added more fuel to the arguments they constantly started about "the mistake she'd made." They'd arranged and paid for a wedding that would have made Scarlett O'Hara proud, supposedly because they couldn't bear the thought of the simple ceremony he and Cynthia planned with their own money, but he knew it was just a ploy to intimidate him. Cynthia was the first to laugh off their concerns about his ability to support their daughter, but he still always felt bad that he'd caused such a rift between her and her family.

When Cynthia died, it was as though her family didn't realize he'd lost someone too. Not a hug from her mother, not a hand on his shoulder from her father. He tried, for Cynthia's sake, to reach out to them, but it was like trying to show sympathy to a brick wall. His relief at their departure was so great he almost forgot his grief. Almost, but not quite.

Cynthia and he had attended the same church for six of their married years, but neither had ever found the time to get involved beyond the occasional desperate call for nursery volunteers or extra manpower for an office move. The pastor did both the funeral and graveside service, but Christian had been almost embarrassed to ask him to, given he didn't remember ever introducing himself to the man. Afterward, Christian stopped attending, and he knew the other congregants, who had probably never noticed them before, didn't miss him. He had his doubts as to whether even God noticed his absence.

Those next few years—well, all the years between then and

now, really—had been pretty bleak. He knew now that he'd built a wall of contempt and anger between himself and God—and even after the revelation of this fact, he still felt a twinge of something sinister toward God as he watched the video of Cynthia dancing on the parquet floor of the country club banquet hall. *Why, God?*

The tape ended and the VCR kicked into rewind mode. Christian stared at the blue screen of the television, still reluctant to leave. He knew he was ready to move on, to leave his life with Cynthia in the past and move forward with Violette into whatever kind of relationship she was willing to enter into, but still there hovered in the back corners of his mind the question of how he would survive if God took Violette, too.

Too much, God. It would be too much. You wouldn't do that to me. Would you?

Violette

The sun is streaming in between the slats of the blinds and casting zebra stripes on the walls. I feel content as Violette snuggles deeper between the sheets. I'm almost disappointed when she gets up and showers.

She walks into the living room where Saul is at the kitchen table with painting invoices, supply receipts, and a notebook of scrawled notations spread before him. "That doesn't look like the work of a computer engineer," she chides as she pours herself orange juice. "What are you up to?"

Saul finishes punching numbers into a calculator and scribbles on the notepad. "Just crunching some numbers here, that's all."

"Bor-ing! The sun's finally out and it's Saturday. We're going out! Get your shoes."

"You haven't had breakfast yet."

"Don't need it. I'm feeding off the sunshine. Let's go!"

"I thought you were going to paint today."

"Well, I *was,* but that was because I thought the sky would still be falling. It's way too nice to be inside the studio. Come *on!*"

Saul sets down the pen and sits back to look at her. He starts to speak, but then interrupts himself. "Okay, where are we headed?"

"I don't know, but we have to eat someplace with outside seating. Did you have breakfast yet?"

"An hour ago."

"Okay, we can get lunch in a couple hours. So…San Clemente will be our first stop."

The roads are packed with weekend traffic, which always seems to annoy Saul. I still don't get why he gets so upset. If you know it is going to be like that, which it always is, what's the point of being irritated by it? It is reality; get used to it—that's my view. Violette ignores the scowl forming on Saul's face and sings along with the radio, rolling down the window and freeing her hair from its ponytail.

Even after their stroll down San Clemente's main shopping street, Saul still seems to be in his own world. Violette taps a finger on his forehead as they wait for their brunch at a sidewalk café. "Hello in there," she sings. "What's on your mind?"

Saul takes a deep breath and swishes his soda with the straw. "Just thinking about…about your painting, actually."

Violette frowns. "You don't like the series I'm doing?"

"No, not the actual paintings. I mean, your painting as a profession."

Violette doesn't like where this is going. "I thought you were okay with me painting full time. Aren't we okay financially?"

"Oh yes, we're fine." He reaches across the table and gives her hand a reassuring squeeze that only partially alleviates her worries. "It's just that…you don't seem to be taking it as seriously as you used to."

Violette almost laughs, but I'm not laughing with her. "What makes you think that?"

"Well, the fact that you haven't finished a piece in nearly three weeks, which is way longer than it usually takes you. And you haven't taken anything new to Xavier in nearly two months."

"Darling, we've only been married for two months. I'm focusing on us right now. Painting will always be there, but the beginning of our marriage only comes once. I want to give as much time and attention to you and us as I can, that's all."

"Well, that's sweet, babe, but you really had some momentum going there at the gallery; I would hate for you to lose it."

She grins. "I didn't think you even noticed that kind of thing. I'm touched. But I still don't think it's as big a deal as you're making it out to be." She pauses. "Was that why you had all my receipts out this morning?"

"Well, yeah… I was looking at your profits from last year, getting everything sorted for taxes, and I started thinking about how successful you were last year. Do you know how much you netted?"

Violette scoffs. "You make it sound like I was fishing or something. I don't even know what netting is, other than the obvious."

"Your profit is your net. And let me tell you, you did pretty well. You really seem to have found a niche, and if we pay attention to what sold and what the appeal was, we can capitalize on that."

Violette sits back and waves a hand in confusion. "You're sounding like a businessman, Saul. You're losing me here. What do you mean, pay attention to what sold and what the appeal was?"

"I mean paint what sells."

"I'm not an artist for hire, Saul. I can't just keep painting the same types of things over and over. That's not how I work. Talk about dull."

"But don't you want to make money?"

"I want to paint what I feel led to paint!" I feel the blood rushing to my face. "I don't do it for the money, Saul. I do it because it's what I do."

"Of course you do it for money, Violette. How else would you have survived before you were married if you hadn't?"

I see Violette's face getting red; the creases in her forehead deepen as her eyebrows knit together in growing anger. I join her frustration, but I try to calm her down so the other patrons won't stare. "I had *jobs,* Saul. I *worked* so I could paint, and if a painting sold, then good for me. But I never *once* painted for the sole purpose of making money."

"What's wrong with that, though? You make it sound like a crime."

Violette folds her arms over her chest. "What are you getting at, Saul? What's the bottom line here? Do I not get to paint if I'm not doing my part to bring in the big bucks? I never pegged you as such a materialist."

Saul leans back in his seat and runs his hands through his hair. "I'm *not* a materialist," he hisses. "I see your potential to be a big name in the art world, and I don't want you to throw it away because you're not disciplined enough to do the work when it needs to be done. And part of the work is painting what people want so you get yourself out there."

Violette catches her breath, and I realize she's suddenly aware of a curious sensation that seems akin to déjà vu. I wonder if she'll be able to see me. She shakes her head and says, "Pay the bill, please. I'll meet you at the car."

She stands and threads her way through the tables on the patio toward the door, and I am pulled along with her. Time fast forwards, and then she's in the car, crying, with Saul beside her. "I was wrong," he says, stroking her hair. "I shouldn't have said anything. It wasn't my place. I'm sorry, Violette." As she hiccups and sniffs and dabs at her eyes with the sleeve of her jacket, he continues, "I just don't approach things the way you do, that's all; I didn't think of it from your view. But now I get it a little more, you know? I understand your side of it. It's just such a different world from what I'm used to. I'm sorry, Violette. I really am."

I feel her swallowing the remains of the lump that had taken up residence in her throat. Violette leans her head on his shoulder and resists the urge to blow her nose on his shirt as revenge for putting her through this. "I forgive you," she mutters. "I don't really want to because you really hurt my feelings, but I can't help it because you're so dang sweet when you apologize."

Saul laughs and squeezes her tight, melting away the last of her resistance. "I am so lucky to have a wife who is so patient with me."

"You've got that right."

"I think she deserves a treat for putting up with me."

I feel my heart soften, and Violette smiles. "Yeah, I think she does too."

He kisses her forehead and starts the car. "That settles it, then. I don't have a choice. I am compelled by your goodness to take you to Taste of Venice."

Violette squeals and throws her arms around his neck. "Are you serious? It's at least a two hour drive—probably more with the traffic."

"I know, but what choice do I have? When you screw up as

royally as I have and make your new bride cry, you can't expect to patch things up with anything less than the best gelato this side of the Atlantic. It's the law of the universe. My hands are tied."

Before she can respond, the scene shifts and we are in Venice Beach. Violette's coffee gelato is oozing down the sides of the cone, and Saul leans over the table to mop a drip from her hand. "You're adorable."

She rolls her eyes in embarrassment. "I eat ice cream like a five-year-old."

"I know; that's why I said you're adorable."

"Should I worry that you find it attractive that I resemble a child?"

"That's not why I find you attractive; it's why I find you adorable. I find you attractive because you're the most beautiful creature ever to walk the earth."

Violette laughs out loud and laps up the drips from the cone. "What are we doing after this?"

"Well, that's up to you. What flavor do you want next?"

Her eyes bulge. "I get two?"

"You get as many as you want. We drove all the way up here, you might as well have your fill."

Violette licks the gelato in the most suggestive way she can muster and winks. "You're going to be *so* happy tonight."

"I can't wait."

"You keep buttering me up and you may not have to. I'm sure

we can find a parking garage somewhere in this city that has an empty floor we can park on."

Saul arches his eyebrows. "How many more gelatos are you gonna eat?"

"Oh, I don't know…two, maybe three?"

"How about one more and then we hit this joint on the way back?"

"Deal. Order me up a chocolate and we can be on our way."

Violette watches him dash to the counter and smiles. But I sigh. I miss my husband.

*I*t was getting easier for Christian to leave Violette's side and venture out during the day. He had started sleeping at home and spending most of the morning at the hospital, then taking the afternoon to go eat, run errands, and give himself some time to think away from the stale air of Violette's room. He made an effort when he was out to think about the world the way Violette did, to look for random beauty and expect the day to be a good one instead of demanding proof beforehand. It kept his mind on things unrelated to comas and the medical world in general.

Today he was going to Violette's house to take in her mail and check on things. Alexine had apparently gone over once before, and Christian felt bad that he hadn't thought to do it himself. He pulled up to the cottage and couldn't help but feel tense at the sight of it. Despite all the time he'd spent here, it was still Saul's and hers.

He walked to the corner and emptied the mailbox. Mostly circulars and credit card applications, as well as some bills and one personal letter. He wondered who the letter was from, realizing there was still a lot he didn't know about her.

Once inside, he opened the windows to air the place out. He sorted the mail on the kitchen table—making a pile each for the bills, applications, and personal mail—then added the items from the stack Alexine had left a few days prior. He threw the circulars in the recycling, pleased that he did know her well enough to know she'd do the same.

It was an eerie feeling, being in Violette's house without her. He hoped the neighbors recognized his car and didn't think him an intruder. He'd never met any of them, and Violette didn't mention them in anything other than a generalized way. It saddened him to think of her being a hermit here on this block. The neighbors didn't know what they were missing.

He resisted the urge to tiptoe from one room to the other. Trying to feel normal, he walked from the kitchen to the two bathrooms, flushing the toilets and running the faucets so the water didn't stagnate. A red 4 blinked on the answering machine in the living room, and he wondered if he should write down and erase the messages to make more room. His finger hovered over the Play button for a few seconds before he moved on. That was a little too personal.

Little reminders of Saul seemed to jump out at him. Framed

photos—Violette in her wedding dress, Saul in his suit; a Hawaiian locale of some sort with Saul standing on a beached surfboard—their wedding album on the coffee table, the stereo equipment Christian could almost guarantee would not have been a Violette purchase. He had the perfect opportunity to clear out Cynthia's belongings when he'd moved to California, but Violette never had that chance. He wondered what else she'd kept.

Feeling guilty, Christian went down the hall to Violette's bedroom and opened the closet. Only *her* clothes. *Good for you, Vi,* he thought. Then he noticed a second closet door on the other side of the bathroom. Expecting it to be a linen closet, he opened it and was stunned at the sight.

Top to bottom, the closet was crammed with stuff. Men's clothes hung from the bar, shoes could be seen scattered among the items on the floor, and the top shelf was bowing under the weight of books and boxes with Violette's handwriting labeling their sides. "Photos" could be seen on many of them. Others said, "Candles," "Mementos," "His office."

He stared at the mess, conflicting emotions battling inside. Part of him completely understood, was even a little jealous; he had so little left to remind him of Cynthia. He began to regret getting rid of so much of her stuff.

Something was leaning against the back wall of the closet. He knelt and pushed aside suit jackets and button-down shirts to get a better look. It was a painting, undoubtedly one of Violette's.

Risking an avalanche, he carefully extracted the canvas and propped it against the wall beside the closet.

It was an abstract, but its subject was clear. The only photos he'd ever seen of the man were the framed ones in the house, yet it was plain from the set of the eyes, the cut of his jaw, and the passion the piece evoked that it was Saul. He'd seen a lot of Violette's work, but he had to admit this was the best, in his uncultured opinion, she'd ever done. Her initials were in the corner, and his heart sank when he saw the date. Only two months ago. She was still painting him with this much emotion, this long after his death, this far into her relationship with Christian?

As quickly as he could without injuring the canvas or upsetting the mounds of stuff on the floor, Christian put the painting back in the closet and shut the door with more force than he'd meant. Sorrow began to descend as he went around the house closing the windows. By the time he got to his car, he was feeling wretched for digging through her things and invading her privacy; he got what he deserved when he found that painting.

He'd let Alexine come from now on.

Violette

June 2000

"W hat are you staring at?"

Violette smiles. "You."

"Why?"

"Because you're beautiful."

"Men aren't beautiful. Unless they're voted so by *People* magazine."

"That's ridiculous. Beauty isn't reserved for women only. Besides, as they say, it's in the eye of the beholder, and that's me; so if I say you're beautiful, you'll just have to go along with it."

Saul laughs and moves up on his elbow to rearrange his pillow. "Okay, so, I'm beautiful. What of it?"

"I want to paint you. Can I?"

Saul's eyebrows jump, and then he laughs. "Oh no. No way, my friend."

"Why not? I won't sell it; this one would just be for us."

"Because it's…it's weird. I don't want to see what your abstract mind comes up with. I'll be all green or something."

Violette laughs and tugs the sheets up to her chin. "You're no fun. But I don't have to have you there to do it, you know; it's not like I don't already have every aspect of your face memorized. I could do it and you'd never know. I was just asking to be nice."

Saul smirks. "You don't have me memorized."

"Oh yes, I do."

"Prove it!"

Violette closes her eyes and throws the comforter over her head. I cannot see anything, but I hear her muffled voice: "Brown, chocolate-kiss eyes, blondy-brown hair with a cowlick on the back and a little lock that always falls down over your forehead, thin nose with a scar on the left side—oh wait, that's my left, your right—from when you had chicken pox, a dimple in your…left cheek, an oval-shaped face and a squared-off chin. You have…let's see…eight freckles: two close together above your…right eyebrow, one by your nose, one above your lip, three on your forehead right near the hairline, and one smack in the middle of your right cheek. You have crow's feet around your eyes, and when you get frustrated a little wrinkle cuts right between your eyebrows." She squishes down a bit of the bedclothes and peeks over the top. I see his beautiful mouth as she says, "And your lips are the color of the inside of a conch shell."

Saul stares at her for a moment before hopping out of bed and going into the bathroom. A minute later he emerges, head shaking. "That's amazing. You're like Rainman."

"No, I'm observant; it's one of my superpowers as an artist. And I stare at you all the time; you just don't usually notice it."

"Well...knock it off."

"Why?"

"Because it makes me feel self-conscious, knowing you're always staring at me. You're like a stalker."

"Can a spouse technically be a stalker?"

Saul thwacks her with a throw pillow. "You know what I mean."

Violette flops over on her side away from Saul. "Fine, be that way, you party pooper."

Saul laughs. "Did you just call me a party pooper? What are we, eight?"

Violette stifles a laugh. "Well, that's how you're acting."

Saul creeps closer. "Well, I'm rubber and you're glue; whatever you say bounces off me and sticks to you. Party pooper."

Violette shrieks as he tickles her, and in the romp that ensues, falls off the bed and lands on her side, her hand bent under her at an awkward angle. I feel searing pain in my left wrist. She screams and rolls over, clutching her arm protectively as tears stream down her cheeks.

Saul freezes. "Violette! What's wrong?"

"My wrist..." She gently lets it go and tries to flex her hand, which only causes her to yelp in pain. "Saul, what if it's broken? This is my painting hand!"

Saul jumps off the bed and yanks on a pair of jeans that were on top of the laundry pile and the first T-shirt his hand finds in the dresser. "Okay, let me get you some clothes, okay? I'll help you get dressed and we'll go to the hospital."

He grabs the first sundress he can find in the closet, then pulls a set of underwear from her dresser. Kneeling before her, he smiles. "I'm pretty good at getting these off you, but I might be a bit clumsy in reverse."

Violette laughs through her tears, but it doesn't last long. "What am I going to do if it's broken, Saul?" she moans as he dresses her, carefully avoiding her arm as much as possible. "I can't hold a brush with a cast on."

"It might not be, sweetie, so don't sweat it. And if it is, it's no big deal; so you don't paint for six weeks. It's not the end of the world."

"Not paint for six weeks?" This nearly starts the tears again. "I haven't gone that long without painting since I started!"

"Well…maybe you'll train yourself to be ambidextrous."

"I can barely hold a fork with my right hand, Saul; I don't think I'll be able to control a brush."

Saul leads her into the living room and pulls flip-flops and a sweater from the closet. "We'll figure something out, okay? I promise. Let's just get this checked out first."

Suddenly I am with Violette and Saul on their way home, the June sun making its way toward the horizon. The clock on the dash reads 2:38, nearly four hours after they left for the hospital. Violette is slouching in the front seat, her left arm encased in fiberglass halfway up to her elbow and a scowl on her face that could ice over Arizona in July. Saul has given up trying to comfort her, and he drives silently down the freeway with the radio on low.

Suddenly I feel my heart lift, and Violette sits up straighter, staring at a building off the side of the freeway. "Hey…"

Saul glances over. "What?"

She cranes her neck, staring over her shoulder as they passed the building. "Did you see that mural on that building?"

Saul nods slowly. "Uh-huh…"

"When you do murals, you don't have tiny details and thin brushes. At least, you don't have to, depending on what you do. You're painting with rollers and broad strokes. I could do that with a cast."

"Have you ever painted a mural?"

"No."

"But it's similar enough to what you do that you think you could pick it up?"

She shrugs. "Why not?"

"Well, what will you need to start?"

"Um…I don't know…some rollers, roller covers, paint trays…"

Then she slouches down again. "But it doesn't matter; I wouldn't have anywhere to paint it."

Saul thinks a moment. "Well," he begins, still thinking as he spoke, "what if…what if we got a big piece of, I don't know, some kind of plain cloth that's not as heavy as canvas—"

"Muslin?"

"I don't know what that is, but sure, muslin. We could staple-gun it to one of the walls of the studio. Maybe put some news-paper behind it so it doesn't bleed onto the wall. Then you could paint on that."

Violette gapes at her husband as he beams with pride. "You're amazing," she said. "That is brilliant. Totally brilliant! I love you!"

He grinned. "So, shall we go to Home Depot for painting supplies?"

"Right now, really?"

"Sure. Then the fabric store for some of that…whatever you called it?"

"Muslin, babe. And yes, if you're sure you don't mind. I know this wasn't how you wanted to spend your Saturday."

"Are you kidding me? Chauffeuring my favorite artist around town as she prepares for the next phase of her career; it's what I've been dreaming of."

By dinner a swath of muslin is stretched taut over the wall of the studio, and an assortment of paint supplies is piled before it.

Despite the throb I can feel in my wrist, Violette battles it out with a thick crayon—another find that doesn't require her to close her fingers as tightly—to sketch out her first mural while Saul makes dinner. "I'm thinking...a giant rendering of your head," she teases as the stir-fry sizzles on the stove.

"Give it up, babe."

"No?"

"No."

"Hmm. Then how about...a field of sunflowers."

"Now that sounds like a really good idea."

"With your face in the center of each one."

He laughs and dumps the stir-fry into a bowl. "You're incorrigible."

"I'm going to paint you eventually, okay? Just get over it."

"Just don't let me see it."

"Even if it's so fantastic that keeping it hidden would be a disservice to the art world?"

He smirks and sets out the plates. "They've lived this long without it, they'll survive."

She wags the crayon at him, squinting. "Just you wait, mister. It'll be the best work I ever do, painting you."

"Oh, yeah? Why is that?"

"Because I love you."

C hristian was on a first-name basis with the staff on Vio-lette's floor, from the night desk nurse to the janitor. He was even to

the point where he could tell who was coming down the hall from the sound of their steps or their voice. They were all nice, all sympathetic to what he was going through, and all pleasant enough to converse with once in a while. But his favorite member of the staff was Katherine, the nurse who came in twice a day to check on Violette and would stay to chat with Violette, or Christian, when she had the time.

Unlike the other staff, who came and went often in less than a minute, Katherine was in for as long as she could spare, curled in a chair or perched on the edge of the bed as she carried on one-sided conversations with Violette. One day soon after he'd met her, Christian had come back from the chapel to find her lounging in one of the chairs with a mug of coffee in her hand and her back to the door as she laid out for Violette the reasons she'd decided to start learning to play golf. Today she was hashing out the argument she'd had that morning with her boyfriend.

"And this is, like, the third time we've talked about this, you know? It's not like this is new information for him. I've told him eight *million* times that he doesn't get to buy me lingerie until I'm ready to let him see it on me, and that's just not happening until the ring's on my finger!" She sighed. "I know what you're thinking, Violette, and you're right! You're totally right. I'm wasting my time with this one. He's got one thing on his mind—don't they all?"

Christian stepped back into the hall and waited until the urge to laugh had finally left him before making a more noisy entrance to warn the woman of his presence. She turned and smiled when she heard him enter. "Hey, Christian!"

"Hey, Katherine. How are you?"

"Not too badly, save for my idiot boyfriend and the grief he's causing me these days. You?"

"Hanging in there."

She cocked her head, scrutinizing him. "Really, you're doing okay?"

He sat down in his chair next to her. "Yeah, well, this is still low on my list of favorite ways to spend my time, but it could be worse."

"That's true."

"So Tim's giving you a hard time?"

Katherine raised an eyebrow. "Men, I swear—no offense."

He laughed. "None taken."

"We've been dating only two months; the man needs to learn some patience." She sipped her coffee and stared briefly into space. "How long have you guys been dating?"

"Almost four months."

"Longer than most of my relationships! How did you meet?"

"She's a painter who does mostly murals these days. I hired her to do one in my office."

She grinned. "Was it love at first sight?"

Christian laughed. "She definitely wasn't what I expected, but in a good way. She's very down-to-earth, albeit with the stereotypical artist streak that predisposes her to odd habits and idiosyncrasies now and then. But we have a lot in common."

"Common ground is good. My boyfriend and I don't have much of that, unfortunately."

"That's a shame."

"Eh, yeah." She sighed. "So how did you two start dating? Did you formally ask her out and all, or did it just sort of evolve from your friendship?"

Christian settled back in his seat, a rueful smile spreading over his face. "Well, it took a little time—and it almost didn't happen, actually. I nearly blew it."

"Really? How?"

"Just being a guy."

"Tell me."

After the dinner where he'd bared his heart and Violette had turned him down, he'd been reluctant to ever talk to her again. He knew it was just his wounded pride, and that hiding from her wasn't going to get him anywhere, but it still took him almost two weeks to call her again. He didn't ask her to dinner again, didn't even try to set up a way to see her. He just called to see how she was doing and if she'd read the article in the paper about the new art installment going in at the Los Angeles Art Museum. His goal was to show her that he could be just a friend, and he figured the occasional phone call would eventually warm her to him enough so he would be safe asking her out again.

They talked for nearly an hour that evening, and when he hung up Christian felt like Superman. He conspired to call again within a week and began racking his brain for reasons. One came in the form of an unexpected conversation with one of the couples he counseled. He had suggested they find something to do together, and one of them made the comment that they'd talked years ago about taking an art class together. Seeing an opportunity, he offered to contact a friend of his who might be able to make a recommendation. When he called her the next day, he did so under the pretense of needing to know where one might go for art classes.

"Branching out?" she asked, laughing. "I pegged you as more of the music-appreciation type."

"Actually, it's for a couple I work with. They want to take an art class together, so I thought I'd see if you had any suggestions of where they should enroll. We're not talking hard core, here; it's really more to get them doing something together."

"Well, let me think." She rattled off the names of a couple possibilities, including her friend, Alexine.

"How about you?" he asked. "Have you ever considered teaching?"

"Oh, no way. I don't have the patience."

"That surprises me. I could see you in a classroom."

"Really? Hmm. I'll have to think about that."

Their conversation meandered for another twenty minutes before she excused herself to make dinner. Christian tossed his phone to the couch, grinning. Another conversation down, another step closer to a face-to-face date.

Violette beat him to the punch the following week when she called to ask if he knew of any good counselors for individuals. "It's for one of the ladies I know at church," she explained. "She thinks she needs therapy." He gave her the names of the counselors his predecessor had referred people to and then managed to draw out the conversation for another half hour before running out of reasons to talk. He was getting ready to say good-bye when she shocked him with a question. "So hey, do you have any plans for Friday night?"

"Um, I... No, not at all," he stammered, scrambling for his Day-Timer. Was she asking him out? "Why do you ask?"

She sighed. "Well, I almost hate to ask, because I don't want to kill you with boredom, but there's this benefit dinner thing for the children's hospital that I've been invited to because I did a mural in their cancer wing. I would just as soon not go, except the guy that got me the gig is a good friend of Xavier's, and he personally invited me to come for the unveiling, so how can I say no, right? And I *hate* to go to these things alone. I asked Xavier, but he's already got something that night, and Alexine's going back East to visit family this weekend. So...geez, I shouldn't have even asked. I'm sorry, that was stupid."

"No, no, I'm glad you did, honestly," Christian assured her. "I would love to go. I'm honored that you asked."

"Are you sure? Because the food will probably taste like cardboard, and they'll probably hit you up for a donation—"

"Violette, relax!" He laughed. "I would love to go. Thank you for asking, and when should I pick you up?"

"Um...six thirty? It's at seven, but Friday traffic from here to Santa Ana is dreadful."

"I hear you. Dress code?"

"Formal, but not black-tie."

"Got it."

"You're *sure* you don't mind?"

"I'm sure."

"You're wonderful. Thank you, Christian."

"You're welcome. See you Friday."

He refrained from shouting when he hung up, but he did allow himself one victory fist-pump as he sauntered into the kitchen to fix dinner. This couldn't be more perfect. He'd bring flowers, he'd get a haircut, he'd rescue her from conversations she didn't want to have, and he'd make up an excuse for her if she wanted to leave early. He'd save her from social hell and be a hero.

He arrived at her door Friday night promptly at six thirty, pale yellow roses in hand. He felt briefly as though he were attending the adult version of the prom and prayed it wouldn't be as awkward. Being suave had never been his strong suit, and he commanded himself not to try to be different from who he usually was. He wouldn't score any points if he ended up sounding like an idiot.

When Violette answered the door, though, all confidence melted. How someone could make a simple silk sheath look suited for royalty was a mystery to him, but there she was, a vision in shimmering spring green, looking for all the world as though she were on her way to Buckingham Palace. Even her usually messy bun looked elegant. He tried to say something normal, but all that came out was, "Oh. Wow. Hi."

She wrinkled her nose. "Too formal, you think?"

"No, absolutely not. It's just...stunning. You're stunning."

An adorable blush crept into her cheeks. "Oh. Thank you. You look fantastic too. I love men in suits when they know how to wear them well, which you apparently do."

The pregnant silence lasted a moment before he remembered the flowers in his hand. "Oh, sorry, these are for you."

Her eyes grew wide and she smiled. "Oh, beautiful, thank you! Come in while I put them in water." She opened the door wider and made her way toward the kitchen before suddenly stopping. "Actually...I have a better idea. I'll be right back." She disappeared down the hall, and he stuffed his hands in his pockets, examining the room and studying the knickknacks that can tell so much about someone: framed pictures of her and a man he assumed must be Saul, a small metal sculpture on the mantle that was too abstract for him to figure out, a desk clock with an antique-looking Roman face. He was about to start perusing the books on the shelf when she reappeared. "Ta-da," she chimed, turning around to reveal the flowers stuck around her bun. "What do you think?"

"Beautiful!"

"They would have lasted longer in a vase, but this way more people can see them before they die and they can have a little adventure." She grinned and picked up a beaded shawl and purse. "Ready?"

When they arrived at the banquet hall, they found themselves seated at the table of honor. Violette clutched his hand as they sat down and whispered, "Thank you *so much* for coming. I could not have done this by myself. I *hate* being the center of attention."

He smiled and winked at her, racing to think of something witty to say when Dale Connors, the chairman of the fund-raising committee and the one who had gotten Violette the job, rescued him. He was friendly enough and kept the conversation going while introducing Violette to other committee members. "This is my good friend, Dr. Christian Roch," she would say when she introduced him. *My good friend.* Not bad at all, he decided. Better than plain old, "This is Dr. Roch." He'd take whatever he could get.

The program began, and Dale welcomed all the attendants and invited them to enjoy their dinners before the program began. Salads and soups were served, and Christian kept an eye on Violette as she was continually engaged in conversation by one person after another, looking for any sign she was overwhelmed or frazzled by all the attention. Whenever these signs appeared, he would jump in and take over for a while, giving her a chance to eat and take a breath. His efforts were always rewarded with a look of pure relief and gratitude, and that was plenty reward for him.

Desserts were being delivered when Dale launched into an explanation of how the funds had been put to use over the previous year. Then a video began which chronicled the changes at the hospital over the past two decades, highlighting the improvements made possible by the donations received over the years. When the lights came up, Dale stepped back up to the podium. "As you know, a children's hospital needs much more than equipment and staff. It needs an ambiance that puts children at ease and hides as much as possible the fact that they're in a hospital and not in a place more comfortable or familiar. Many of these children find themselves spending more time at the hospital than at home, and because of that, we have been focusing greatly over the last year on making the areas more cheerful where children tend to stay for longer than a week. One of those, the cancer wing, recently received a face-lift in the form of a beautiful mural painted by Violette Corterm, who is seated here to my right as one of tonight's honored guests." The applause began, and Violette rose briefly and gave a quick bow of thanks. "The mural was finished just three days ago after almost two months of work, but we managed to put together a short 'video unveiling' for all of you so you could see not only the quality of this piece, but also how it has already helped to brighten the lives of the children who get to see it every day."

The lights dimmed and Christian could hear Violette sigh. "This is so embarrassing," she whispered to him as he repositioned his chair to better see the screen.

"This is a huge honor, Violette, you should be proud!"

"I'd rather be under the table."

He stifled a laugh and squeezed her shoulder as the video began. As the story opened, Violette was kneeling before the wall and sketching out shapes under the watchful eye of two bald girls who stood just beyond her. The next scene showed her outlining the shapes in paint and chatting with a little boy in a hospital gown and baseball cap. It was followed by a shot of four children each dabbing paintbrushes on the wall where Violette pointed for them to paint, which inevitably turned into dabbing each other with paint. As the audience laughed, Christian felt a surge of pride for Violette. He wished he could show her how impressed he was by her spirit.

The video went on, including interviews with some of the children guessing what the mural would be when it was done and showing where they had helped Violette paint. The video ended with a shot of the completed mural, which depicted children playing in a field of flowers. Some of the children's faces in the mural were covered over with mirrors, and when the video ended Dale went back up to the podium to explain. "When Violette first showed me the sketches of the mural, I was confused as to why some of the children's heads were empty ovals. 'Those will be mirrors,' she told me. 'Children can look in the mirrors and see themselves playing in the field. Visualization is a powerful healing tool, so I wanted to help the children on the ward to be able to visualize themselves outside those walls and in a place where they could run around and just be kids.' And they do just that. The doctors on the ward tell me that kids hang out in the hall all the time, moving from mirror to mirror to picture themselves out in that field that Violette has so masterfully created. Please help me in thanking her for her tremendous work."

People began to rise to their feet, applauding and whistling their appreciation. Once more, Violette, greatly embarrassed, stood and thanked the crowd. Without thinking, Christian reached to squeeze her hand, and she held on for dear life as the applause went on. Once it finally died down, Dale got underway with his pitch for donations, and after outlining the financial goals they hoped to meet for the upcoming year, he wrapped up the evening and released the audience to fill out their donation cards and mingle. Almost immediately, a dozen people wanting to commend her on her work approached Violette. Christian stood beside her and wrapped a protective arm around her waist; she immediately moved in toward him as though trying to escape the crowd. He could tell that after fielding questions and saying "thank you" a hundred times, she was on the brink of a meltdown.

Christian lifted a hand and cleared his throat. "I'm sorry, folks, but we need to go." Violette smiled apologetically to the people around her and allowed Christian to lead her from the group. She thanked Dale and grabbed her shawl and purse, then followed Christian out the door to the lobby where he turned over his claim ticket to the valet.

Violette heaved a massive sigh. "You are a lifesaver."

"I was afraid you'd explode if you had to stand there much longer with all those people crowding you."

She laughed. "You're right. I can't thank you enough."

The car came and they got in. "Straight home, or would you like to get some coffee or something?" Christian asked, begging *want coffee, want coffee* in his head.

"I think just home, if that's all right. Those people wiped me out. Is that all right?"

Christian masked his disappointment. "Of course! Home it is."

The ride was mostly quiet, with only an occasional remark. Christian went over the evening in his mind, analyzing all he'd done and coming to the conclusion that things had gone very well. By the time they reached her house, he was already trying to plan what his next move would be and how long he should wait before taking it, feeling very certain that things were moving in the right direction.

"So what's your next job?" he asked as he walked her to the door.

"I have two possible clients I'm meeting with next week, but nothing other than those. I'm going to take a little time off, maybe paint some canvas pieces again. I have a couple ideas in my head, but haven't had time to sketch them out yet."

"Well, good luck on those."

"Thanks. And thanks again for coming tonight."

"Any time, Violette."

"No, really. That was so above and beyond, and you were so supportive. I would still be there if it weren't for you—although I'd be on the floor in the fetal position by now."

He laughed and moved to hug her, and she kissed him on the cheek. It was just an average peck, nothing serious, but it was enough to send a shock through his system. When she stepped back, he could see the blush on her cheeks by the porch light. "Sorry," she said quickly. "I don't know what I was thinking."

He shook his head. "No, don't be." Then, energized by this show of affection, he silenced the warning bells in his head and kissed her full on the mouth.

For a moment he got the distinct impression she was kissing back. Then suddenly she stepped away, a look of surprise on her face. "You kissed me."

"Yeah, I did." He let out a nervous chuckle. "Didn't expect that, sorry. Just...sort of happened."

"I can't believe you did that."

This wasn't going well; he could tell by her face. "I'm sorry, Violette, I really am. If that hurt you in some way, I apologize; it was not at all my intention."

"Well then, what *was* your intention?"

Christian stepped back and took a breath. "I...don't really know, Violette. I guess I was just...hopeful that the kiss on the cheek was a muted expression of how you were feeling. I took a chance, and apparently I was wrong." He wanted to kick himself. "If I've really screwed something up here—"

"You have."

He blinked.

"Christian, I'm not ready. I *told* you that."

"I know you did, but I thought maybe that kiss was—"

"It was a show of gratitude, that's it." Her face was red.

"Correct me if I'm wrong, but you *did* kiss back for a second there."

She was silent, and her gaze dropped.

"I'm right, aren't I? I wasn't imagining that part."

"I don't know." Her voice was so low he could barely hear her. "I guess you're right."

"Well, then, there you go," he countered lamely, trying to keep the emotion out of his voice.

They were both silent, neither looking at the other, until finally Violette pulled her keys from her purse. "Good night, Christian."

"Wait, Violette. I don't want to leave things like this." She sagged against the door and stared at him with a helpless expression. He rubbed his eyes. "It *didn't* ruin everything, Violette. It was a kiss, between friends, and while I would love to think there's more of that in our future, I *know* you're not ready. I jumped the gun, and I'm sorry. I read more into your peck on the cheek than was really there because I *want* there to be something. But you're not ready, and that's fine. But I'm not embarrassed by it, and if you felt like kissing back, you shouldn't be embarrassed, either."

"But Saul…"

"Saul's dead, Violette."

She grimaced, irritated. "I *know* that."

"In your head, maybe, but not in your heart."

Violette started to speak, then shook her head and unlocked the door. "Good night, Christian." He saw the tears in her eyes when she left him standing on the porch.

Katherine got a good laugh out of Christian's story. "I wouldn't have pegged you as the kiss-stealing type."

"Shocking, huh?"

"You can say that again." From the hall came the sound of someone calling her name and she sighed. "Well, I'll have to hear the next installment later. My time's up for now." She stood and patted Violette's hand. "Bye, girlfriend. See you later."

She waved to Christian, then headed out the door.

Violette

$\mathcal{I}$ have been trying so hard.
We've been married for over
a year. The adjustment has been difficult at times, though well worth it,

and I am proud of the compromises I've been willing to make for
Saul. My tendency toward being a night owl is curbed so Saul and
I can go to bed together and share breakfast in the morning. My
natural bent toward independence has been readjusted to where I
hardly mind having someone in my space all the time. My craving
for solitude finds fulfillment in the hours Saul is at work and I have
the place to myself to paint.

We moved into a small house three months after the wedding, and Saul did his share of compromising too. Instead of making the guest bedroom an office, we made it my studio, and he
turned the garage into his own personal space. I'd been itching to
paint every room of the house, and he willingly allowed me to

choose all the colors, even when they weren't quite what he would have picked.

But, even still, we've each screwed up at times. A blowout usually ensues, tears are shed (me), and doors are slammed (Saul). Eventually the dust clears and we realize that the problem has more to do with understanding each other than with the small matter that caused the explosion in the first place. And as Violette sits at the kitchen table, staring at the pile of bills before her, I have a feeling she is heading for one of those times.

I would be the first to admit I am not the most organized person in the world, nor the one with the sharpest memory. But I'd been working at it, because I wanted to show Saul that, despite the way I sometimes acted, I really am a responsible adult. I had a feeling he thought Alexine had been the one who had taken care of details like bills and home repairs when we'd been roommates. And while this just so happened to be true, it *wasn't* because I was not capable, but because Alexine had a knack for those things—mainly, she remembered to do them.

So I had created a very organized approach to the bills, complete with color-coded folders and a hand-decorated box in which to keep the checkbook, stamps, address labels, and bill-paying pens. I'd shown off my new system to Saul and asked him to let me take over that particular responsibility, which he had surprisingly agreed to. Truthfully, I'd expected a little more reticence on his part, and was almost disappointed that I hadn't been forced to resort to my list of reasons why I was more than capable for the job.

That was six months ago, and up until now things have been going swimmingly. But a snag in the system has appeared, and Violette isn't sure what has happened.

After we moved into the house, we found an antique armoire that was tremendously out of our price range, but gorgeous, and if we chose to finance the charge, we wouldn't have to pay interest until after a year. We calculated how much we'd need to pay each month in order to pay the whole thing off before the interest charges kicked in, and that's what we'd been paying. Yet, the bill is in front of Violette, and the amount left to pay is far, far more than it should be.

"Okay. Don't panic," she tells herself as she holds the statement in her trembling hand. "This is obviously some kind of mistake. By the bank. Not by us, because I *know* I've paid this bill every month." She flips back in the check registry and counts up the payment just to make sure—and yes, she's made five payments in five months. Just as it should be. So what is the problem?

She calls the customer service number on the statement, trying not to freak out over what is certainly a bank error. Surely these things happen all the time. *"Small mistake, so sorry ma'am, we'll take care of that right away."* And then she can tell Saul how she's caught a huge snafu that nearly cost them a thousand bucks. He'll be so proud of her.

After five minutes of hold music that nearly drives her to physically harm herself, a bored voice comes on to ask for her account number. Once it is squared away that she is who she says she is, Violette launches into her complaint.

"Let me take a look at your payment history," the bored woman says, and the hold music comes back, eliciting a groan from Violette. After a minute the woman returns. "According to our records, your January payment was late."

"But you got it, right? So what does it matter?"

"Late payments render the interest agreement void."

I feel like I've been punched in the gut. Violette drops the purple ballpoint she's been tapping nervously on the table. "Since when?"

"It's all in your account agreement, Mrs. Corterm, under Interest and Finance Charges." Violette sits still in the chair, stunned. Her mind is racing. What has she done? "Is there anything else I can do for you, Mrs. Corterm?"

"No, thank you," she mumbles weakly before hanging up and dropping the phone back in the charger. This can't be. It just can't.

She jumps up so quickly the chair falls over, and she sprints out the door to the garage where Saul keeps all the important papers in his filing cabinet. Taking the key from its hiding place, she unlocks the cabinet and yanks out the drawer that holds all the credit card agreements and papers for the house. A file marked *Armoire* in Saul's blocky handwriting is stuffed toward the back. She pulls it out and falls into his desk chair, then begins to methodically remove each paper. The one with the interest and finance charge information is easy to find. She carefully reads each word, then reads each word again and again.

The woman is right. It's right here, section four, part C. Legalese isn't my forte, but Violette understands the gist of the message: pay late, pay the interest charges. *All* the interest charges.

"Oh no, oh no, oh no," she murmurs to herself as she stuffs the papers back in the file and the file back in the cabinet. She slams the drawer shut, locks it, and replaces the key. She runs back into the house and flops on the couch, and I am depleted of energy. Saul is going to kill her.

Eventually she drags herself back to the table, rights the chair, and pays the rest of the bills. Not knowing what else to do with the one for the armoire, she pays the amount they usually paid, then tacks on an extra hundred dollars to try to eat into the interest. After stamping and labeling all the envelopes, she takes them out to the mailbox, then retreats to the bedroom where she buries herself beneath the sheets and awaits Saul's arrival from work.

He comes home an hour later, calling for her the minute he is through the door as he always does. She wipes away the tears that have been trickling from the corners of her eyes and prepares to face her doom.

"Why are you hiding in here?" he asks when he pokes his head in to look for her. "Are you okay?"

"I really screwed something up," she sniffs. "You're going to be really mad."

"Oh, babe, come on. I won't be mad." She raises an eyebrow and he shrugs, as he sits next to her on the bed. "Okay, I'll probably get a little mad, but I always get over it and we're always okay, right? So no big deal. What's up?"

She sits up and takes a deep breath; then, avoiding his eyes, mutters, "I made a payment late."

"Okay."

"On the armoire."

"Okay."

"And now we have to pay the interest charges because we missed a payment so there's a ton more on the bill for what we owe and I'm really, really, really sorry."

He is trying really hard not to get too angry. "How much more is a ton?"

"One thousand thirty-seven dollars and forty-nine cents."

"One thousand?" His voice is louder than she expected it to be. She nods, feeling the tears start again. "Why was the payment late?"

"It was the January one, when we went to New York—I forgot to do the bills before we left, and when we got back that one was late."

"*Just* that one?"

"Um…well, no, a couple of them, but—"

"How many?"

"I don't know, two or three maybe?"

"Three? Which ones?"

"Saul! Back off. Geez, what does it matter?"

"It matters if it puts a dent in our credit rating!"

"Oh, come on, one late payment isn't going to—"

"Look, whatever. Just put your little bill box and folders in the garage, and I'll take care of it."

"Take care of what, the interest charges? I don't think there's anything we can do about it. I read through the credit agreement."

"No, the bills. I'll take care of the bills." He stands and walks out of the room, leaving Violette fuming. When she realizes he isn't coming back, she untangles herself from the sheets and goes after him. "What do you mean, take care of the bills?"

"What do you think I mean, Violette? I'll do them."

"I just did!"

"I mean from now on."

"What?" I feel the heat on my face, and her voice cracks with anger. "I screw up once and you're giving up on me?"

"Well, what do you want me to do? Wait until you've missed a mortgage payment and we go into default?"

"What makes you think I'll screw up again?"

"Because you're—" He stops and his mouth snaps shut.

Violette stands, hands on hips. "I'm what, Saul? Go on, say it. You're thinking it and that's just as bad, so you might as well say it. I'm irresponsible? I'm immature? I'm too flighty?"

"Forget it. I take it back. You can have the bills."

Violette throws her hands in the air. "I can't believe you!"

"What? I gave you back—"

"It's not about the bills! Do you have any idea, Saul, how hard I've been trying to be all organized and responsible for you?"

"It's not about me, Violette—"

"Of course it is! Why else would I be doing it, you idiot? I was doing great the way I was, but obviously that wasn't working for you, so I *tried* to be Miss Responsible. And for five months I did just fine, and I didn't even get so much as a 'Hey, thanks for taking care of the bills' from you. But the second I screw up, you hit the roof!"

Saul is gripping the kitchen chair so tightly his knuckles are white. "Well, Violette, I'm sorry. I'm sorry you screwed up. I'm sorry you just cost us a thousand bucks. I'm sorry I never told *you* thank you for doing something that you never thanked *me* for doing. I'm sorry for thinking maybe you were ready to start pulling your weight."

She gasps. "*What?* Pulling *my* weight? You think I'm freeloading off you? You think I'm just hanging out here during the day doing nothing? I'm trying to cultivate a new skill, trying to build a new part of my career…and I'm sorry if I can't just take a couple classes like you can to advance in my job. But I guess I shouldn't be surprised that you feel like this. You've never seen my art as a real career. You've never taken it, *or* me, seriously, have you? I can't believe I ever thought you'd be able to. Your mind is way too narrow to ever accept me and what I do. *Why* did I even *marry* you?"

I want to bury my face in my hands; instead I'm watching Violette and Saul stare each other down as their fight escalates. When he finally storms out of the house, slamming the door behind him, Violette falls onto the couch, sobbing. I want to get back in my body, but I don't know how I got out in the first place. After a few minutes I watch Violette rise and look tentatively out the window, then walk to the bedroom and pull out a small suitcase. I have a sense of foreboding and try to stop what is happening, but again cannot figure out where I am in relation to all the action.

Violette throws random clothes from her dresser into the suitcase, muttering under her breath the whole time, then zips it violently and carries it to the living room. Grabbing her keys and backpack, she leaves the house without bothering to lock it and tosses the suitcase in the passenger side door. I am right behind her the whole time, aching to stop her and powerless to do anything. I am being carried off to Alexine's as Violette weeps and drives.

"I should have known, Lex," Violette cries to her friend. "I should have known he'd never get it. How could I have been so stupid?"

"You're not stupid, Vi. He's always been a gentleman. This just came out of the blue."

"Well, now what do I do?"

Alexine folds her legs up beneath her. "I don't know. Maybe

you should talk to the pastor at church. Isn't that the kind of thing pastors are supposed to help with?"

Violette shrugs. "I dunno. I guess. But Saul wouldn't go there with me."

"He doesn't need to; just go and find out what they think *you* should do."

"I guess you're right. I'll go tomorrow."

"Are you hungry?"

"Starving."

"Chinese?"

Violette smiles, mopping up the remaining tears with the edge of her T-shirt. "Yes! The usual, with extra egg rolls."

"You've got it." Alexine picks up the phone and dials a number from memory as Violette goes into the kitchen.

She stands at the sink, staring out the window as she sips some water, trying to shake a feeling of déjà vu, when the doorbell rings. "That's the fastest delivery I've ever heard of!" she calls out to Alexine.

She hears Alexine chuckle and go to the door. "Yeah, right. If it's Girl Scouts, you want to order a box?"

"Heck, yeah."

Alexine scampers into the kitchen and hisses, "It's not Girl Scouts. It's Saul."

Violette nearly drops the glass. "I don't want to talk to him."

"Are you sure?"

"Yes. Not yet."

Alexine disappears into the living room again, and Violette hops up onto the counter in the far corner of the kitchen, staying as far from the doorway as possible. She hears the door open and Saul's voice waft through. "Hey, Alexine. Can I see Violette? I assume she's here."

"She doesn't want to talk. I'm sorry."

"She told you what happened?"

"Yes, she did. You screwed up big time."

Violette stifles a giggle. Go Alexine!

"I know, I know. I just want to apologize. Can you ask her if she'll just come out for a minute?"

"I can ask, but I'm not forcing her, and you're staying outside." Violette hears the door close, and then Alexine appears in the doorway. "He wants you to come out so he can apologize."

"I know, I heard."

"And?"

Violette sighs. "I don't want to."

"Then don't."

"But I probably should."

"Then do."

"You're no help!"

"Hey, I'm not married. I don't know what the rules are."

"Same as when you're dating."

"Then break up with him and don't take him back until he comes begging with flowers and chocolates."

Violette can't help but smile. "Okay, so it's not *entirely* like dating."

Alexine leans against the pantry door. "Look, are you going to forgive him eventually?"

Violette twists her wedding ring on her finger as she thinks. "Yeah, I guess so."

"Well, then maybe you should just go ahead and do it now and get it over with so you can move on with your life."

"But I'm still mad!"

"Well…that's okay, isn't it? Tell him you're still angry but you forgive him. You can still stay here tonight if you want to."

"You sure?"

"Of course! I like impromptu sleepovers."

Violette chuckles. "Okay, I guess I'll go talk to him." She hops off the counter and takes a deep breath as she walks to the door. Squaring her shoulders, she flings it open and steps out onto the balcony. Saul is leaning against the railing, staring down at the parking lot below, and barely even moves when she comes out. Mimicking his posture, she positions herself a couple feet down the railing from him, avoiding his eyes the way he avoids hers, and waits for him to talk.

After a few moments of silence, Saul finally speaks. "I'm sorry."

"I'm listening."

"I...I was insensitive."

"Yeah, you were."

"I shouldn't have exploded at you the way I did."

"I agree."

"It was an honest mistake that you made, and I blew it way out of proportion."

"Exactly."

"But in my defense, I wasn't in my right mind at the time."

Violette arches a brow. "How so?"

"I found out today that I might get laid off."

Violette claps a hand over her mouth. "What? What happened?"

Stuffing his hands into his pockets, Saul leans on the railing and looks at her. My heart melts at the sadness on his face. "They announced today that our company is getting bought out and they're letting half the employees go. I'm one of the youngest in the department, in terms of how long I've been there. Chances are I'll be the first to go."

"But you're so good at your job!"

"Yeah, well, so are the other guys."

"Oh, honey, I'm so sorry." Forgetting her anger, Violette wraps her arms around him and nestles against his chest. "No wonder you were so upset."

"I'm just worried about finding a new job and how we'll make it financially if I'm out of work for a few months. They'll give us a severance package, but it won't be much, and now that we have a mortgage and all—"

"I understand, sweetie. I totally understand."

"But that doesn't excuse what I said about you pulling your weight. You do exactly what you've always done, and I've never had a problem with it before. I should have been grateful for you wanting to take some of the house responsibilities off me."

"Well…yeah. I'll give you that." They laugh. "But at the same time, you do so much that I never thank you for, so that I *can* be free to do my thing. So thank you."

He smiles. "You're welcome."

"And if I need to get a job for a while to help out, I can do that too. I don't mind. Just let me know."

"That's sweet, babe. Hopefully it won't come to that."

Alexine pops her head out the door. "Should I order more food or will I be eating alone?"

Violette grins at Saul. "Hungry?"

"Starving."

"Why don't you call in another order of sweet and sour chicken, Lex?"

"Consider it done."

When the door closes, Saul plants a kiss on Violette's forehead. "So are we okay now?"

"I think so."

"Do you still love me?"

"Immeasurably and unendingly."

"Okay, good."

"How about you? Do you still love me?"

"Yeah, I'm pretty fond of you."

"Thought so."

"Wanna make out?"

Violette laughs. "On the balcony?"

"Not on my balcony!" comes Alexine's voice.

Saul's eyes twinkle. "Tonight. Our bedroom. Be there."

"You're on."

There were strangers in the room when Christian arrived that morning. Five men and women of various ages—though none looked older than midthirties—were standing around Violette's bed and holding hands. One of the women, a petite brunette with a pixie haircut and the longest earrings he had ever seen, was praying aloud while the others would "mmm" and "amen" their agreement. He'd never seen someone pray with that much authority or confidence; if it weren't for the humble language, he'd have assumed by her tone that she was used to bossing God around and getting what she wanted.

He stood in the doorway as they prayed, trying to pray along instead of studying the individuals crowded around the bed. When the pixie-haired girl, finished another woman began to pray, then after her one of the men. He was the last of them, and when he concluded his petition they all added their amens to his and opened their eyes. One of the women spotted Christian in the doorway and smiled. "You must be Christian!" she exclaimed. The others turned and smiled, offering hands to shake and, in the case of the pixie-haired girl, bypassing his outstretched hand altogether and moving in directly for a hug.

"I'm Dana," she said. "We're from Church in the Canyon."

"Oh, Violette's church. Of course. A pleasure to meet you."

"We were here a few days ago," said one of the men. "The nurses said you were usually here, but we must have missed you."

"Oh, yeah, I'm sort of in and out. It's very kind of you to come, though. Thank you."

"Of course. I'm Noah Long, one of the pastors. We're the prayer team from CitC." He pulled out a business card and handed it to Christian. "If there's anything we can do, praying or other-wise, please call me. We'd love to be able to help you and Violette."

"Thanks. I really appreciate that."

"So how is she?" This from one of the other women.

Christian shrugged. "Okay, I guess."

"Do the doctors give any indication how long this may last?"

"No, there's no way for them to tell. Two to four weeks is typical, though, and she's been here almost a week, so..." Christian shrugged again.

"We'll try to come every three days or so, but if something happens in the interim that we should pray about, please let us know."

"I will."

Noah looked around at his team. "On to the maternity ward we go, then!" He grinned at Christian. "One of our members had a baby last night after four miscarriages, so we have some celebrating to do. Care to join us? There's a cake and coffee up there."

Christian shook his head and smiled. "Thanks for the offer, but I think I'll pass. Give my congratulations to the mother."

Noah shook his hand again, as did the others, and they began to file out of the room. Dana was the last to leave. Again she hugged him, then stood back and looked at him with a curious stare. "I'm going to pray for you," she stated.

"O-oh. Well, um, thank you," he stammered.

He thought she meant later, or at home, or in her head, but she took one of his hands in hers and placed her other hand on his shoulder. "Father God, we praise you for your provision and the strength you give us to face the perils of this world. I ask for peace and grace upon Christian as he waits with such steadfastness by Violette's side. Reward his loyalty and guide his steps as he and Violette face the challenges of the future. Draw him ever closer to you and calm the questions of his heart. In the name of Jesus, your beloved Son to whom we pledge our lives. Amen." She released him and smiled up at him wordlessly before disappearing out the door.

Christian stared after her in stunned silence. No one had ever prayed for him like that before. And no one had ever prayed for just the right things without him articulating what his needs were.

He made his way slowly to the chair he always occupied, mulling over the words she'd prayed, and sat down heavily. "Quite a group of friends you've got over there," he muttered to Violette. He grasped her hand and gave it a squeeze, then picked up his journal from the table and opened it to the next blank page.

"Calm the questions of my heart?" How did she do that,
God? Did you tell her that, or is my inner turmoil written
in sixty-point font on my forehead? There are questions,
all right:
> Will she live?
> Will she be the same?
> Will I love her if she's changed?
> Will she ever love me back?
> Will I be able to forgive you if you take her away?
> That last one is paramount, God, and I'll admit it,
I don't know if I could.

He'd relished that morning at his home when the clouds had parted in his head and he felt hope restored to him. He knew he couldn't assume that hope equaled the outcome he wanted. It could mean hope for his own relationship with God. Hope for the strength to deal with a postcoma Violette who was not the same as the one he'd loved before. Hope for the state of his own aching soul. But if God didn't come through for him the way he was praying, he couldn't guarantee he'd even want God's hope anymore. He couldn't see himself wanting anything to do with him at all.

Christian closed the book and placed it back on the table. Sometimes the journaling helped, other times it muddied the waters even more. When it led him to more frustrations and unanswerable questions, he set it aside to deal with later.

He was staring off into space when Katherine's face appeared in the doorway. She peeked around the doorjamb before entering, a sheepish grin on her face. Christian couldn't help but laugh. "You look like you're expecting trouble."

She laughed. "I came by earlier but there were a bunch of people here. I think they were praying over Violette or something."

"Yeah, they were. Friends of hers from church."

"It was a little creepy."

Her smiled. "Yeah, it actually kind of creeped me out too."

"You're not into the church scene?"

"No, I am, actually, but just not the same scene as Violette's. My church is a lot more..." He realized any way he ended that sentence sounded wishy-washy to him. It probably wouldn't to Katherine, but to someone who had an inkling of what an active relationship with God was like, his reply would belie a disdain for the passion some had for God. "A lot more private," he finally said. "How about you? Do you go to church?"

"No, not really. Christmas Eve and stuff, but that's about it." She avoided his eyes as she spoke, concentrating on the notations she made on Violette's chart, and Christian could sense her discomfort with the topic.

"So, how are things with you and your boyfriend?"

She rolled her eyes and gave him a rueful smirk. "About as steady as a drunk at last call. I foresee a split in my future."

"I'm sorry to hear that."

"Eh, well, I'm not, frankly. He's wearing on me. I don't need a boyfriend that makes my life more confusing, you know?"

"Understandable."

She waved her hand. "Enough about him; he's not worth it. I want to hear the rest of your story about how you and Violette made it past your tremendous faux pas. I still can't believe she didn't at least slap you or something."

Christian laughed. "I don't think Violette's the slapping type. Actually, I can see how she might have been in the past, but from what I gather from our conversations, I think she's mellowed a bit. But I agree she deserved to hate me for a little while."

He hadn't bothered to call her after that night. He was so embarrassed at his behavior—acting like some hormone-riddled teenager who reads permission into every flutter of a girl's eyelashes—that he couldn't bring himself to face her even over the phone. And while he wasn't totally fluent in the rules of dating, he was pretty sure he'd forfeited his right to make the next move anyway. So the ball was in her court, and from what he guessed, it was going to sit there on the ground, untouched, possibly forever.

Christian set about squelching any hope he had for a friendship, much less a relationship, with Violette. After a few days, however, he realized how hard it was to let go. She had become his main source of peer interaction—he had no friends to speak of, no family in the area. So he swallowed his pride and got out the yellow pages, looking for a church that sounded somewhat similar to the one he had attended with Cynthia. It was the one thing he'd "never gotten around to" after moving to California, and if he was going to meet people he could remotely relate to, he figured he'd have to take the leap. The next Sunday he hauled himself down to Beachside Community Church, and after the service, which he decided he'd be able to tolerate on a weekly basis, he signed up for a singles' outing to an Angels game and for a men's intramural basketball league.

The night of the Angels game was only mildly disastrous. Ten people showed up, only two of them women, and Christian was stuck between one of them and a baseball-obsessed guy. The woman was an introvert who didn't get the basics of carrying on a conversation, and the guy was concentrating on the game so he could fill out the play chart in the program. He gave up trying to talk with either of them by the end of the second inning, which made the next seven painfully long.

The intramural basketball team started the following week. He wasn't the oldest guy on the team, but he was definitely the least athletic, having last played on his frat's intramural team in college. By the end of the first practice, he doubted he'd be in shape for the game that weekend; when he woke up the next morning, he doubted he'd make it to the car to go to work. He ditched his usual hour of patient review to soak in the tub and limped into work just as his first client was arriving.

A week passed, then a second. A third. A fourth. Still no word from Violette. By that point he'd gotten used to the thought of never seeing her again. He'd attended Beachside Community for a month, had weathered two more singles' events and emerged virtually unscathed, and had scored two baskets for the church's basketball team. He'd even gone on a date with a woman he'd met—not in the singles' ministry, surprisingly—and had a decent time, although not decent enough to go out with her again. But it gave him hope. Decent women certainly lived in Southern California, and he was bound to find one he connected with.

A message waited on his answering machine one evening when he came home. The sound of Violette's voice nearly knocked him off the couch, and he had to play it again after he missed half of it because he couldn't concentrate on what she was actually saying. "Christian, hi. It's Violette. Listen, I wanted to see if you were free sometime this week or next for coffee. Give me a call when you get the chance. Bye."

He was stunned. He'd finally stopped thinking about her,

about just how unlikely it was they'd ever get together, and here she was. He noticed, though, that once the shock wore off, it was not replaced with the giddiness he'd felt toward her before. He wasn't scrambling to call her. He wasn't planning out what he'd say. He wasn't plotting how he'd approach their meeting. He wasn't even considering it a date.

He ate dinner before calling her, then finally dialed her number. She answered on the first ring, unusual in his experience with her, and the tone of her voice brightened considerably between "Hello" and "Oh, hi, Christian!" Still, he didn't get his hopes up.

"Got your message," he said simply. "How does Thursday sound?"

"Sounds great. Where shall I meet you?"

"Java Jax's on Main? I have clients until eight, so I can meet you around eight thirty, if that works for you."

"That would be perfect. How have you been?"

"Not bad. You?"

"Um...okay, I think. Pretty well, actually. I'm looking forward to talking to you about it."

Despite himself, his curiosity was piqued. "Well, I look forward to hearing about it. See you Thursday night."

By the time he was pulling into the Java Jax parking lot, he'd lost all the control he'd cultivated over the weeks of non-Violette communication. Back was the giddiness, the plotting, the hope.

He almost hated himself for it, but oh well. He wasn't about to screw up again by being aloof. If he was being offered a second chance, he was going to take it.

She was already there and had staked out a table by the window. He caught her eye and waved before placing his order, then took his seat across the table. "You look really nice," he said, although he'd wanted to say she looked absolutely gorgeous and ask what the occasion was, because she had definitely gone the extra mile. Her clothes *and* hair had been given attention, and he'd never seen both coordinated at the same time. Even for the benefit dinner she'd done nothing special with her hair, other than stick the rosebuds in it, and halfway through the evening it had been falling out all over the place. But tonight it was down, with some curl in it, which he didn't remember seeing before, and not a spot of paint was to be seen on her clothes. His years with Cynthia had trained his eye for makeup, and he'd noticed early on Violette never wore any—but tonight he was pretty sure he detected some eyeliner. What was going on?

"So it sounds like things are all right," he started off. No sense in beating around the bush, especially when she'd hinted so blatantly on the phone.

"Yeah, I think they are," she said with a shy smile. "And I have you to thank."

"Really? I'm flattered. What did I do?"

She stirred her coffee with a swizzle stick and stared as the cream swirled on the surface. "You told me Saul is dead."

Christian cringed. "That was a little harsh. I'm sorry about that."

"No, no, I mean it. That was what I needed to hear. The harshness is what probably helped. I mean, enough already, you know? It's time to move on."

He held up his hand in protest. "Now, Violette, you do realize that it's okay to still be attached to him, right? I don't want for you to have misinterpreted my statement. Attachment without stagnation is possible, if that makes sense."

"Completely. And I agree. And I think I'm there."

Christian stuffed the counselor side of himself into a box. He'd done his part; now it was time to act like a potential boyfriend and not like a potential therapist. "That's fantastic, Violette. I'm really happy for you."

She grinned. "Thanks. I'm happy for me too."

"And I'm glad something good came out of that evening."

"Oh, are you kidding? Tons of good! I mean, besides the fact that you kicked me out of my rut, you also gave me the first kiss I'd had in two years. How could I fault you for that?"

Christian was embarrassed and hoped it didn't show on his face as much as he felt like it did. "Well, you know me—always happy to help." He raised his coffee in a mock toast and grinned.

"Regardless, I hope you know I really did feel awful about that. I was so out of line, especially for a relational therapist."

She laughed. "Hey, at least I know you're not ruled by your job. That's a good thing."

"Yeah, well."

Violette tucked her hair behind her ears and leaned on the table. The gesture was distinctly adolescent, but in a good way—in a young-at-heart way. Christian liked it; it suited her. "So, if you remember, you agreed way back when to help me celebrate when I felt like I was ready to move on."

"I definitely remember."

"Then what do you say to a date?"

"I say absolutely. Name the day and time and I'll be there."

"Tomorrow night, whenever you get off work."

"Tomorrow is—oh man, believe it or not, tomorrow doesn't work. I have basketball."

Violette laughed. "You have *what?* Since when do you play basketball?"

He didn't quite feel comfortable saying, "Since I had to find ways to get over you," so he went for the only-slightly-misleading answer. "Well, I started going to this new church and they have a guy's intramural team. I played in college and thought it might be good exercise."

"Are you any good?"

"Actually, no, I'm pretty terrible."

She was enjoying this. "Well, maybe I should come watch you."

"Oh, please don't," he begged. "I'm afraid you'll lose all respect for me."

"Okay, okay—Saturday night?"

"That works for me."

"Six thirty?"

"Perfect. Why don't you choose the restaurant too?"

She smiled. "All right then, Castleman's in Laguna Hills."

"You've got it." They toasted and filled the next hour with easy conversation, and by the time he was back in his car Christian felt like a new man.

Three weeks later, though, he wasn't sure what was going on. He and Violette had gone out six times for various engagements—dinner, movies, coffee—but it still wasn't clear to him where their relationship stood. The most physical contact they'd had was a hug or two at the end of an evening and the occasional hand on the arm during conversation. He wasn't about to risk another kiss, as much as he wanted to, and while beggars can't be choosers, he wanted to know what was different between now and their friendship before. Maybe he'd misread her intentions—maybe this wasn't the path to a relationship, but the lame purgatory of "just friendship."

But, he had to remind himself, this was a big step for her, and maybe she was just a little gun-shy. Not that he could blame her, given the way he'd misread her before. Maybe she was afraid to show too much attraction, too much affection, in case he took it as a license to throw himself at her again. Maybe she just needed a little more time.

"A little more time" turned into another month, and still nothing changed. Postdate embraces (if they were dates at all) continued to be the standard fare, and no terms of endearment were bantered around. He was all for taking things slow, especially in the wake of emotional and relational tragedy, but this was getting ridiculous. He wasn't sure if he had a girlfriend or just a friend who was a girl—and if it was the latter rather than the former, then he wanted to know so he could plan accordingly.

He decided to give her one more week. That would make two months of quasi-dating, and certainly after that long he was justified in initiating a discussion on where things were going.

They went to dinner, and this time he raised the bar a bit. Nicer restaurant, predinner drinks at the bar, and a small gift to commemorate two whole months of their new...whatever it was they had. That would segue perfectly into what he wanted to talk about.

After they'd ordered dinner and the menus had been cleared away, Christian reached into his pocket and pulled out a small box. "This," he said with a flourish, "is for you."

Violette's eyes grew wide and she beamed. "You bought me something?"

"I did."

"Why?"

"Well…that's a good question. Open it first and tell me if you even like it."

She tugged the red ribbon from the small white box and pulled off the lid. Judging from the way her expression went all melty, he was pretty sure he'd chosen well. "Oh, Christian, this is just beautiful!" she gushed as she pulled the bracelet from its cotton bed. "Will you put it on for me?" He reached across the table to attach the clasp, and she gently fingered the tiny silver shapes adorned with hand-painted flowers. "Where did you get it?"

"I will never reveal that bit of information," he chuckled. "Now that I know you like it, I have a whole store of guaranteed bull's-eye gifts. If I tell you where it is, you'll go buy everything and I'll be at a loss next time I want to get you something special."

She laughed and settled back in her seat. "So what is the occasion?"

He took a deep breath and launched a quick prayer. "Well, today marks two months since we started to"—he paused and waved a hand—"do whatever this is we're doing. Dating, seeing each other, hanging out."

Even in the low light he could see her blush as she caught his meaning, but he didn't want to put her on the spot too much, so he moved on. "Anyway, I thought that deserved some celebration."

"Well, that…that was very thoughtful of you." She toyed with the ribbon from the box. "I happened to be thinking about that very fact this morning—the fact that it's been two months. I was proud of myself."

"And well you should be."

"And I was trying to figure out where I thought things should go from here."

Christian's stomach knotted in anticipation. "Good. I'm glad we're on the same wavelength." He exhaled.

Violette let out a nervous laugh. "Yeah, well, after two months I'd hope we are at least in the same wavelength vicinity." She set the ribbon aside and sipped her wine. "I think I'd like to be…man, this is so awkward," she muttered. "I feel like a teenager."

Christian reached across the table and took one of her hands in his. "I know *I* would like you to be my girlfriend, if you think you're ready for that." He smiled. "Was that anywhere near the wavelength you were on?"

Her eyes darted from his face to their hands resting together on the table, and a slow smile took over. "Yeah, it was."

"So it's official then, eh? We're a couple?" He wanted to cheer, but he restrained himself. "And you're okay with that?"

She nodded. "I think so, yeah. We're official."

He kissed her hand, then released it and sat back in his seat. "Well, that's a relief, because that store has a ton of stuff I know you'd love, and I would have been really disappointed if I'd had no use for any of it."

She laughed and spun the bracelet around her wrist. "So... have you dated anyone since Cynthia?"

"Not really, no. Occasional dates here and there, but no relationships."

"So you're not going to be any help for me as I muddle my way through this, huh?"

"Well, not from experience, no. I can dispense the textbook theories and tell you what worked for my clients, but that's about the extent of the help you'll get from me. Other, of course, than the utmost support and understanding."

"Better than nothing, right?"

"And better than doing it alone."

"True. I'll give you that."

Christian raised his glass. "Well, then, here is to muddling through together as an official dating couple." He frowned slightly. "Is it just me or does the word *dating* sound really adolescent?"

She raised her glass and tapped it to his. "Yeah, a little, but what else is there?"

"Hmm, good point. We should come up with something new."

"Well, you're on your own there. I'm an artist, not a wordsmith."

At the end of the evening, he drove her home and walked her up to her door. Standing with his hands in his pockets, he grinned. "I'm not going to try anything, I promise."

She laughed and hugged him. "You're such a gentleman."

"Yeah, usually."

She stood back and scrutinized him for a minute, then went up on tiptoe to plant a quick kiss on his lips. "More than usually." She smiled and let herself into the house. "Talk to you later, *boyfriend.*"

Katherine laughed. "That's so cute!"

Christian grinned and stood to stretch. "Well, maybe so; but unfortunately the story doesn't end there."

She sighed and stood. "Well, unfortunately, I need to get going. I can't wait to come back, though; it's story time with Dr. Roch. Will you be here when I come around later this afternoon?"

"Actually, I don't think so. But I'll be here tomorrow."

"Will the praying people be back?"

He chuckled. "I don't think so; but they don't bite, you know."

"Yeah, I know, I know. All right then, I'll talk to you tomorrow."

Christian watched her leave and then moved to Violette's side. Taking her hand, he kissed it and held her knuckles to his forehead. "I have to say, love, if we make it through all this, we have a heck of a story." He stared down at her for a minute, the psychologist in him itching to get in her head and see what was going on, then gently placed her hand back at her side and left to get some coffee.

Violette

*V*iolette awakes to a noise she can't identify. The sunlight is streaming in the window, and the clock reads 7:24. I see her sit up and rub her eyes, trying to wake up. She is alone in bed. "Saul?"

October 2002

A vague panic is pulling at her heart, and she doesn't know why—but I do. She thinks back to the night before, knowing she's not forgetting some traumatic incident. Just dinner and a movie and a wild romp in bed before succumbing to sleep after two in the morning. She thinks maybe that's why she feels panicked: she hasn't slept nearly enough. "Saul, where are you, babe?"

The panic isn't going away, and Violette's hands begin to shake. A shadow takes over her thoughts. Violette throws the covers off and flings open the bedroom door. "Saul?"

I remember. As much as I'd hoped to avoid this memory, I haven't, and I remember it all. At the end of the hall, the studio

200

door stands slightly ajar. A piece of glass shimmers on the wood floor just in front of it. I've never had much glass in there; just my water jar, really, and the occasional drinking glass. Violette's heart is beating so loudly I can hear it. She knows something is wrong.

"Saul, what's going on? Are you here?" She steps carefully to the door, watching where her feet go in case of more glass. She reaches her hand out to open the door further and freezes. *No!* I scream silently.

Violette hesitates, and I am afraid my fear is transferring on to her. But then, without giving herself a second longer to think about it, she shoves her hand forward and pushes open the door.

Saul is lying face down on the floor, a vase shattered next to him with the bouquet of flowers and broken glass jumbled in a pool of water. Violette screams as she falls to the floor beside him and jabs a trembling hand to his neck.

I am sobbing. "Not again, not again," I moan. "I can't live this again. Not again!"

Violette sweeps her arm across the floor to move the flowers and glass away, then suddenly staggers to her feet and lunges for the phone on the desk. "My husband! Please, help me, he's dying!" she sobs to the 911 operator. She gives her address and then drops the phone to the floor, carefully rolling him over and placing an ear to his chest. "Oh God, oh God, please!"

Violette curls up on the floor with her head on his chest. "God, please!" we both cry. The sound of sirens outside startles Violette, and she scrambles to get out of the way as paramedics burst through the front door. Within seconds the house is filled with uniformed men and women, and Violette is gently led to the living room while the paramedics work. I am in the living room with them, despite how badly I want to be in the studio. I try to move back in, but can't—it is as though I've forgotten how to walk.

Saul is wheeled out of the studio on a stretcher, and Violette is ushered out after him by one of the police. They put her in a squad car and follow the ambulance to the hospital. All the while, Violette stares out the window, unspeaking, ignoring the comments being made by the police in the front seat. I am empty.

Once at the hospital, Saul is whisked away, and a nurse who writes down the information Violette is able to provide patiently questions her. When they ask who they can call for her, the name Alexine and her phone number roll off her tongue without her even needing to think about it. When she asks where Saul is, all they say is, "They're going to do everything they can for him."

Violette stands by the nurses' station, waiting for Alexine while watching the minute hand on the wall clock slowly tick its way through time. Ten minutes pass, and she can't take another second of staying in one place, so she begins to wander the hall. Movement in one of the closed-off rooms catches her eye. She walks toward it, and we both know Saul is there. "Not again, not again," I murmur to myself. Four doctors stand around the bed, but there is no flurry of activity like there should be. I feel heaviness inside me as Violette wonders why they aren't doing anything anymore. "Oh God, please, oh God, please…"

Doctors stand back, glancing at machines.

"Oh God, please, oh God, please…"

A hanging of heads, the stripping of gloves.

"Oh no…oh God, please, no…"

Heads turn to look at her through the crisscrossed glass. Her husband's body, now fully in view, is unmoving. Alexine's arms suddenly come around her. "Vi, what's happening?"

A doctor breaks away from the cluster and makes her way to the door. Violette's eyes lock with hers, and Violette begins to shake. Alexine holds her tighter.

"Mrs. Corterm?"

"Oh God."

"I'm Dr. Wallace…"

"My husband…"

"I'm sorry, Mrs. Corterm."

With those words, I am united with Violette again, and my body slumps down into Alexine's arms with a gut-wrenching sob.

I am curled on Alexine's couch. After calling Saul's parents and my father with the news, I collapsed. Alexine left me alone, occasionally bringing a glass of water or plate of crackers to set on the coffee table, but nothing more. I don't touch the food, though, and have remained silent. Without bothering to ask, Alexine drove over to the house to bring back some clothes and toiletries and, I suspect, to clean up the evidence of the morning's events. Now that she's back, I hear her on the phone. A sliver of me is curious about what she is saying, to whom she is talking, but not enough to find out.

It gets dark. I watch the sky fade to black, then stare at my reflection in the window. Alexine comes in and out, cooks in the kitchen, curls up for a while in the armchair with a book, then eventually stands and drapes a blanket over me before going off to bed.

I do not sleep, though. I stare at the ceiling for a while, then get up to nibble on the crackers and to stretch. My body aches from being still for so long, and I wander slowly from the living room to the kitchen to work out the kinks. All alone, I know I won't be confronted with conversation, so I feel more like being up. I make a sandwich, then return to the couch and click on the television—not so much to watch as to have something else moving in the room besides myself.

Saul's parents will take care of the funeral. I don't care what it's like or where it'll be. The only thing consuming my mind right now is the idea of going home and if I will be able to bear it.

I wake when Alexine walks from the kitchen. The television is off. Alexine smiles at me. "Hey."

"Hey."

"Can I get you anything?"

"No, thank you." I feel as though I'm made of cardboard: flat, emotionless, inanimate.

"Is there anything you want to do today?"

"No. Can I stay here, though, for a couple days?"

"Are you kidding? Of course you can."

"Thanks."

The shadow of a person moving in front of the window prepares us for the ring of the doorbell a moment later. Alexine peeks out the peephole. "It's Xavier." She opens the door and he enters with a bright pink pastry box.

"Oh, sister," he says simply, then pulls me into a hug as he sits on the couch. "I brought donuts. Small consolation, I know, but I didn't know what else to bring."

"Any chocolate long johns?" I ask.

"Three."

"You're my hero." I feel my stomach rumble as I open the box and pull one out. Donut poised at my mouth, I pause. "Is it awful that I'm eating a donut when my husband has just died?"

"Honey, is this not what comfort foods are for?"

Justified, I cram half of it in my mouth as Alexine brings in milk and napkins from the kitchen.

We eat in silence for a while, then I speak. "I don't know how I'll ever be able to go in my house again, much less the studio."

"We'll ease you in, Vi; don't worry." Alexine pats my knee.

"And you're an artist through and through; eventually it'll get to the point where you just can't put off painting anymore. That'll help."

I appreciate Xavier's words, but I seriously doubt he is right. I can't imagine anything dragging me back in there again.

I am home. I've been here for a week. Alexine is staying too, asking me every day if I feel like cleaning through the house to remove some of the more painful reminders of Saul. Every day I turn her down. I'm not ready to let go of anything yet.

One morning when Alexine wakes up, I tell her she can go home whenever she wants to. "Are you sure, Violette? Because you know I'll stay if you want me to."

"I know you would, and that's why you're the best friend anyone could ask for. But no. You need to live your life, and I need to figure out how to live mine without the training wheels."

Alexine hangs out for the rest of the day. We go grocery shopping and out to lunch, then splurge on pedicures before going home. We watch one of the movies we've seen together a million times and eat popcorn and trail mix until it gets dark. Then Alexine stands, hands on hips, and stares me down. "You're sure about this?"

"Yes."

"Call me if you need me."

"You know I will."

I lock the door behind her and quickly turn on the television so the room won't be so quiet. I turn on every light in the house, except, of course, in the studio—the door to which is closed and even barricaded with a chair from the kitchen. Then I start sweeping, then dusting, then vacuuming, then mopping the kitchen floor—not because the place really needs it, but because I can't think of anything else to do. Staying active seems better than going to bed.

At three in the morning, I collapse, exhausted, on the couch. I want to sleep in my own bed, but I'm suddenly afraid to be in there when the house is empty. "This is ridiculous," I say aloud. "Go to bed. You've slept in there for a week now without a problem." I march down the hall and into the room, which is ablaze with light like the rest of the house. "See? No big deal. You're tired, the bed is comfortable, just go to sleep." Without bothering to change out of my clothes, I crawl under the covers and fall almost instantly asleep, with all the lights still on.

*W*hen Katherine came the next day, she didn't even let Christian start the small talk. "I need the rest of the story—this is better than *All My Children.*"

He didn't feel much like telling the story today. He'd spent the evening before mulling over how it was all going to end, and he didn't like the endings he came up with. The more he thought about their relationship and the past few months, the more he realized something was going on with Violette that she'd never said anything about.

Being a therapist, he was usually pretty good at looking past people's words and actions and seeing the hidden meanings behind them. But he'd so desperately wanted to believe that Violette was truly ready for their relationship to progress that he'd willingly shut off his therapist's intuition and ignored the blatant signs. To yet again rehash all the signals he'd missed—and in front of an audience—wasn't exactly what he wanted to do.

His hesitancy made Katherine look up from her work. "Oh. Not such a happy chapter in the story?"

"Well, it's not as tragic as this chapter, that's for sure." They exchanged sympathetic smiles. "But you know what they say about hindsight being twenty-twenty?"

She chuckled. "Oh yeah."

"Well, that's what this part is like."

"Ah, I gotcha." She sighed and hooked the chart back onto the foot of the bed. "Well, I can't force you to talk about it, but…I'm not going to let you leave me hanging, either." She winked and settled into the other chair. "So as long as I get to hear the rest eventually, I don't care when it is."

He laughed. "So I'm not off the hook?"

"Nope."

"You're a cruel woman."

"Me? Naw," she scoffed. "Just a curious one."

Christian stood and stretched. "All right, all right, you win." He rubbed a hand over the back of his head. "Well, let's see…"

They'd been officially dating for three months. Frankly, it wasn't too different from when they were friends, except he got to kiss her now. It wasn't quite what he'd envisioned, but then again, it's not as if they were teenagers with raging hormones. They knew what they were missing, as it were. He just hadn't been in the dating game at this age before. Maybe that's why things weren't what he'd expected. He didn't know what *to* expect.

But looking back, he could see that he'd ignored her hints. She would never make the first move to hold his hand, kiss him, or hug him, although she never shied away when he would make the advance. She rarely called him unless he'd left a message, but once on the phone they could talk for hours. And the L word…well, that was a whole other story.

Christian was pretty sure he loved Violette. He hadn't known her long, but he'd loved Cynthia and knew the feeling. More importantly, he knew the risk and the sacrifice, and he'd already decided Violette would be worth it.

But was he about to say it to her? No, because her language toward him, her behavior, sent a standoffish vibe. So instead of speaking his feelings, he exhibited them through the little gifts that he bought her and the time he spent with her.

It took an innocent remark from one of her church friends to bring Christian somewhat to his senses. He surprised Violette at one of her mural jobs when his last client of the day canceled and found her chatting away with the woman who'd gotten her the job at her daughter's elementary school. Something about the look in Violette's eyes when she saw him walking down the hall made him refrain from greeting her with the kiss he'd planned, which irked him. To cover for his frustration he slapped on a smile and shook the woman's hand as Violette introduced him. "Norah, this is Dr. Christian Roch. Christian, Norah Fleming; she's one of my friends from church."

"So nice to meet you, Norah."

"You as well, Christian. How do you know Violette?"

A red flagged waved, but he soldiered on. "I'm her, ah, her boyfriend."

Norah's eyes bugged. "Violette! I didn't know you were dating anyone! And here I was scheming for a way to set you up with my cousin. That would have been embarrassing."

Christian chuckled along with her, swallowing his anger over Violette's three-month cover-up of their relationship. Why hadn't she told anyone?

They bantered for a few more minutes before Norah excused herself, and once he was confident they were no longer within hearing range of anyone that mattered, he fixed Violette with a hard stare that made her wither. "I'm sorry," she finally groaned. "I'm sorry, Christian. I…I don't know what else to say; stop staring at me."

"You haven't told anyone at church that we're dating?"

"N-no."

"You volunteer on a serving team, *and* you're in a Bible study, both of which mean you're discussing your life with people on a fairly regular basis, and yet you haven't told *anyone?*" She avoided his eyes and began instead to clean up her supplies. "Well, that certainly puts me in my place, doesn't it? At least now I know where we stand."

"Christian…"

"What?"

She sat down amid her supplies and hung her head for a moment before finally shaking her head. "Nothing, never mind." She began throwing things into her bag willy-nilly and stacking the paint trays and cans into the laundry basket she used to transport them. Christian watched her, wondering what to say when so many things were crowding onto the tip of his tongue, but then she was slinging the backpack over her shoulder and hefting the basket and leaving. He ran beside her and took the basket from her, which she wordlessly allowed, and in silence they went to her car to pack her things away.

"Let's go talk," he said as they closed the hatchback.

"I don't really feel like it."

"Violette, I really think we need to talk about this."

"I'm sure we do, but we don't have to right now. I need to go home." She flung open the car door and slammed it behind her before Christian could protest. His anger overshadowed all the other emotions he was feeling, and he got into his own car and followed her home, lecturing her in his mind and occasionally aloud. He pulled into the driveway behind her and caught up with her as she was wrangling the laundry basket through the front door. "Go away, please," she said through clenched teeth.

"No, Violette, this is ridiculous; take five minutes and tell me what's going on."

She disappeared into the studio with the basket and emerged a moment later, still avoiding his eyes. "I'm not up for this right now, Christian; just leave me alone."

"That isn't how relationships work. You can't just brush me off, especially not after what just happened."

"Well, that's what I'm doing, so you'll just have to accept it."

"No! We either talk about this now, or we end it now. I don't want to be with someone who doesn't respect our relationship enough to be honest when there's something going on."

She froze and finally looked at him, eyes blazing. "Are you giving me an ultimatum?"

The silence was painful. He finally filled it with an emphatic, "Yes."

The staredown didn't last long. "Fine. Good-bye." Violette turned and stalked to her bedroom. The slam of the door echoed down the hall and into the living room, where an astonished Christian stood until the air had purged the sound of Violette's anger. He walked to his car, feeling slightly unsteady, and drove himself home.

Violette

*I*t took some effort to get myself to go to bed that first night after Alexine went home, but now that I'm here, I'm having trouble getting out. All my energy is drained; all motivation and desire to do pretty much anything have completely disappeared. I spend the better part of each day in bed, alternating between sleep and unfocused staring at the walls. I venture out for food once in a while, but only choose that which is quickly prepared and eaten— cereal, toast, granola bars. Then back to bed.

Alexine calls now and then, and I politely endure telephone conversations; but I gently turn down any offers to go out or have her come over. Xavier does the same, going so far as to show up on my front step. I let him in and allow him to trail me back to the bedroom, where he reclines beside me and fills an hour with one-sided conversation about the gallery and his dating escapades while

I huddle beneath the covers. Eventually he gets the message and leaves.

Sometimes I think about Saul, about our marriage, about the house that feels like a big cave now that it is just me wandering through it. Every now and then I leave the bed and sit on the couch or on the floor in the bathroom or at the kitchen table and stare at all the little things that bring back memories: the framed photos from our wedding and honeymoon, the burn mark on the wood floor near the stove where Saul dropped a flaming dishtowel, the seashell salt-and-pepper shakers he bought for me at the beach. My eyes fix on the objects, but my mind fixes on the memories until I'm barely aware of my surroundings. When my mind comes back to the present, the shadows have crossed the floor, or the sun has set or risen, and I shuffle back to bed, disoriented from the time shift.

Sometimes I cry. The tears come out of nowhere, unprovoked; I stare at nothing, huddled beneath the comforter, and tears begin to trickle from the corner of my eye. Or other times I see something I haven't noticed before—one of his favorite pens sticking out from beneath the couch, or a box of Chicken in a Biskit crackers, his favorite snack, at the back of the pantry, and the next thing I know I'm sobbing in a pile on the floor. Sometimes I sleep, and my dreams are convoluted and worrying, and I wake up in a sweat without knowing why. Or I don't dream at all and sleep away twelve hours at a time.

Week two passes pretty much the same way. Week three as well. Week four something happens that I don't expect: I get visitors. And not Alexine or Xavier, either. The doorbell rings and on the front steps stand four people from Church in the Canyon.

I've gone there for a few years now, although not on a regular basis, and I've never gotten that involved. Other than occasionally volunteering to help decorate for the holidays or fill in now and then as a greeter at the door before a service, I've never gotten connected. But I recognize all of them, including the guitarist from the worship band and the décor coordinator.

I'm conscious of how awful I must look but not motivated enough to do a whole lot about it. "Hold on a sec!" I call, then pull on a sweatshirt and sweatpants and yank my hair back in a ponytail. I swish some mouthwash around for a couple seconds, then open the front door.

"We've missed you, Violette!" says Sandie, the décor lady, as she gives me a hug. I let them in, despite wanting to tell them to leave, and I try to figure out how to get rid of them quickly.

"We hadn't seen you in a while, so we wanted to come by and see if there was anything at all we could do for you." This was from Billy, the musician.

"Thanks," I reply. My voice sounds rusty, as though I'm getting over laryngitis.

"Are you sick too?" asks another lady. I think her name might be Dana.

I feel a tickle in my throat. I cough. "No, just not talking much these days, that's all. Been a hermit lately."

"I understand." Dana's apologetic smile makes me want to punch her.

The other person, Cole, looks around. "So, what do you say, Violette? Can we get you some groceries? clean your house? pray with you? Honestly, we just want to do whatever you need done. We know how hard this must be for you."

No you don't, you inane idiot. "Actually, I'm good. A couple of my friends come over now and then to help me out with stuff. I'm fine. In fact, I can't think of anything you could do. But thanks for coming over." *Please get the hint.*

"You know, if you don't want to socialize right now, I totally understand that," Billy says. I hope the relief isn't too obvious on my face. "But at the same time, we really felt like God prompted us to come over here and...I don't know...do *something*." He shrugs. "So if you want to just go back to bed or whatever, that's fine with us, but would it be okay if we maybe just hung out here and prayed for you?"

I'm too stymied by the request to tell him off. "Uh, I-I guess," I stammer. "Are you serious?"

Dana nods. "Yes. We won't push you or anything, and like he said, you don't even have to hang out here with us. But if it's okay with you, we'll just sit out here for a little while. And if you want to join us, great. If not, no worries."

Feeling very uncomfortable, I throw up my hands and mumble, "Yeah, whatever, that's fine. Thanks." Then I retreat to the bedroom.

Once safely entombed in my room again, I try to sort through the mad swirl of emotions that has overtaken me at the sight of these people and the declaration of their intentions. They want to *pray* for me? God *sent* them? What kind of cockamamie story was that? The nerve of them to ask if they can just sit in there when I clearly do not want company. They are sick voyeurs, like the rubberneckers who slow down to ogle a car wreck on the freeway. They just want to see grief up close.

After I allow myself to rail against them in my mind for a bit, I calm down enough to admit that they probably aren't voyeurs and probably they're just trying to be nice. And they are being nice—I just don't feel like having anyone be nice to me right now.

And the whole God thing. I've been avoiding that can of worms since Saul's funeral when the minister from his family's church had babbled some crap about it being Saul's time and how lucky he was to be in God's presence. If God didn't approve of Saul being in *my* presence, he shouldn't have allowed us to meet in the first place. He didn't have to go and kill him just to get him away from my influence.

Truth is, I started taking the God stuff I heard at CitC somewhat seriously in the months before Saul died. Parts of it still made no sense to me, but the general idea of a God who loved me definitely had its appeal, and the concept of allowing an all-knowing

God to guide me seemed logical. If someone has the map, then why travel blindly when he can tell you where to turn?

And I liked Jesus—a nonconformist in the truest sense, but rebelling for more pure reasons than any of the nonconformists I'd hung out with in school, and obviously much wiser. Some of his stories were a little out there, but the lessons he taught resonated with me, and I appreciated his guidelines for living.

CitC talked a lot about what it meant to be a "Christian"—or a "Christ-follower," a term I liked more than the former because it has a more hippy feel and doesn't smack of the traditional. They talked about *surrender* and *salvation* and *atonement* and *redemption,* big words that I liked the sound of but hardly understood. They talked about loving others, which I liked, and about absolute truth, which I wasn't so sure about but was willing to consider. They welcomed Xavier the one time he came to see my handiwork in the decorating department, which made me happy, though I hadn't yet been able to nail down exactly what they thought about homosexuality.

Yes, I'd been right on the edge of jumping in to see what this faith had to offer—and then God had to go and ruin it by taking my husband.

And now he is supposedly sending an envoy to check up on me or something. Is that his way of trying to declare a truce? of trying to apologize? *Sorry, God. A motley collection of well-wishers is a bit inadequate.* I want nothing to do with a God who plucks people randomly from the earth and excuses it as "being their time." No one as young and healthy as Saul could be anywhere near his time.

I planned on not going back to CitC ever again—and now CitC is coming to me. I'm not sure how to handle that.

The sound of voices can be heard in the living room. For fifteen minutes after I retreat to the bedroom, I hear them talking, then they fall silent and I hear the door open and close. Just as I am relaxing at the thought of being alone again, I hear the voices pick up and the door opens and closes once more. What's going on? A strummed guitar chord answers my question. Billy brought music. How nice.

I know better than to expect something off the radio. My suspicions are confirmed when he begins to play the intro to one of the worship songs I'd heard at church. He's being respectfully quiet—as quiet as one can be when playing a guitar—and when their voices join in, I have to strain to make out the words I'd heard only a few times.

I am baffled. What exactly did they hope to accomplish? I'm not going to be charmed out of my room by music—heck, Billy is the only one who sounds like he can really carry a tune—and if they think it might be soothing, they're wrong. The words I can remember or understand while they sing just grate on me. What is all this about a God who loves, a God who cares? Yeah, right. Whatever—that hardly explains why I have a king-sized bed all to myself.

They sing three songs, then pray some more. I hear shuffling that indicates they might all be finally leaving. Footsteps down the hall stop at my closed bedroom door, and Dana's soft voice calls, "See you later, Violette. We love you." I don't answer. I wait until the door is closed and the sound of a car pulling away breaks the silence of the fall afternoon. I feel my body go limp as I give in to relief, knowing they are no longer camping out in my living room, and I quickly go to sleep.

A week later the doorbell rings again. This time the CitC people have the guitar right out in the open, and Sandie is holding a Scrabble box. I don't even bother being polite this time. "I don't really want visitors," I state bluntly as I clutch my robe shut.

"We understand," Dana says, and they all nod in agreement. "But it's not good to be alone so long. You don't have to hang out. We just want you to have some people around."

"Why?"

"Because God didn't design you to be a hermit."

"Well, forgive me, but I don't care at the moment what God designed me to be or not be. I'm in a bit of an anti-God kind of mood."

"I don't blame you. Look, last time we were here, I saw you had a table on your back patio. Could we hang out there and play?"

I shake my head in amazement and open the door wider. "Yeah, fine, whatever." I leave them at the front door and stalk back to my room, irritated at their sympathy and compassion and Scrabble. A few minutes later the guitar can be heard, but not the typical strummed chords of a worship tune. It sounds like Billy is just playing—no voices accompany him, and his approach sounds more like that of one who is killing time or filling dead air than someone purposefully playing. The chatter of conversation wafts in with the music. It's like listening to a picnic.

I huddle deeper beneath my blankets, but can't entirely shut out the happy sounds from the backyard. Eventually I give up and decide to eavesdrop instead. Trading my pajamas for sweats and a T-shirt in case I am spotted, I creep out of my room and down the hall to the window that faces the backyard and sit down beside it. Scrabble discussion dominates the conversation—comments about scores, the existence of proposed words, and the Christian version of trash talking—and over it all is Billy's meandering guitar.

They play for an hour, then begin to pack up. I scamper back down the hall to the bedroom before they come through the house to leave, and again ignore Dana's farewell from the other side of my closed door. But after they are gone, I find myself wishing, ever so little, that I'd joined them.

Three days later they are back, and this time I don't even stick around to talk. I simply open the door and say "Come on in" in a voice thick with resignation, then go back to my room and close the door. But instead of jumping into bed, I sit on the floor with my ear to the door, listening to see what they are doing this time.

They have brought a movie. I don't know which one, but I hear discussion about the volume and finding the VCR remote. A few minutes later music sounds from the television and curiosity gets the best of me. I open the door as quietly as possible and tip-toe down the hall until I can see the screen. Gwyneth Paltrow is running down a street in a business suit, and credits are blinking occasionally onto the screen. I ease myself to the floor and lean against the wall, being careful to stay out of view of those who are apparently sitting on the couch just on the other side of the wall. The title of the movie, *Sliding Doors,* appears, and I am mildly pleased. I'd wanted to see this movie when it first came out.

Time flies. The ending shocks me, and I stuff my fist into my mouth to keep from crying out loud and getting caught by the others. When it appears to be over, I scramble back to the bedroom before Dana comes for her usual good-bye.

I have mixed feelings. On one level, I am truly annoyed that these people insist on busting into my personal space and imposing on me. But they are being so casual about it, so passive-aggressive, that I have to give them credit for trying. It isn't a bad approach, really. Frankly, it's working better than they know. But I resent being pulled out of my shell before I decide on my own to emerge.

Never more than a week passes before they come back for another visit. Sometimes it's games, sometimes it's movies, and sometimes it's prayer. One time it is dinner made from scratch—each person comes in bearing a plastic bag from the grocery store—and the smells that float into my room nearly do the trick of enticing me out. A grateful "Thank you!" actually escapes my lips when Dana announces from the hall that they are leaving the leftovers in the fridge. As soon as the coast is clear, I am in the kitchen and eating the first full meal I've had in weeks.

Sometimes I am secretly glad for their presence. Other times they catch me on a bad day, and I sit in the bedroom praying (not to God specifically) for them to leave. The days that they pray make me even angrier. I want to run in and shout, "Why are you even talking to him? Don't you see what a sadist he is? How can you worship a God who would do this?" But mostly I hide out in my room with my ear against the door, or huddle in the hall and listen to their conversation, or watch the movie they bring. I wonder if I'll ever be open to their God again.

As the months pass, I spend less time in bed and more time in the living room, lying on the couch or sitting at the kitchen table. The minute anyone comes to the door, I withdraw to my bedroom, but generally I have regained the desire to roam the house. Except, of course, the studio. I haven't opened that door since moving home from Alexine's after the funeral. Alexine told me she cleaned up the mess left behind from the Event We Never Name, but that isn't enough for me. The image of Saul on the floor is indelibly etched in my mind, and I'll never be able to walk into that room again without seeing it.

"Would it help if the room looked completely different?" Alexine asks over egg rolls one night.

I shrug noncommittally. "I don't know. Maybe. It would have

to be drastically different, though—not just new paint on the walls or a new area rug, you know?"

Alexine nods thoughtfully. Then after a moment she asks, "Could X and I take a crack at it?"

"At what, redoing it?"

"Yeah."

"How?"

"How would we redo it? I don't know. I have a vague idea, but I'd have to talk to him first."

"What are you thinking?"

Alexine smiles. "It's a secret. If we decide not to do it, I'll tell you what it was."

I throw her a pouty glare. "Well, just remember, I'm not making any promises. It may not matter what you do."

"I know, I know."

Secretly, though, I hope it *will* help. I haven't held a paintbrush since the day before The Event, and while I'm not exactly itching to start again, I also don't like the forced ban. When Alexine announces she and Xavier have come up with a game plan, I feel my eyelid twitch, and I have to bite my lip to keep from crying.

"Here's the deal, though: it's going to be a surprise, so you've gotta stay out of the way."

I hear alarm bells going off in my head. "I don't want to leave the house."

"You don't have to. Just stay in your room when the studio

door is open. We'll work with it closed most of the time and warn you when we need to come out."

I shudder. "I don't want to see it anyway."

"Well, there you go. We'll start Saturday."

Xavier and Alexine appear at my door with boxes of supplies. I try to take a peek into them but am rebuffed. "All in good time, love," Xavier responds. "Don't spoil the surprise." I watch them disappear around the corner into the hall, hear the studio door open and shut behind them. The squeak of the door makes my stomach leap. I still cannot imagine walking in there again; the thought of it makes me sick. I retreat to the kitchen, feeling guilty that they are spending all this time and energy and money on me, and try to figure out what to make them for lunch.

They emerge four hours later with random smudges of green and tan paint on their clothes and faces. I grin playfully. "You're wearing clues," I tease. "Let's see, what's green and tan…"

"Don't bother. You'll never guess," Xavier chuckles.

"And if you do we'll have to kill you." Alexine quips. "We'll have you in there soon; just be patient."

I frown. "I still don't know if I even *want* to be in there."

"Trust me, it'll be wonderful. You'll love it. You *do* like plaid and paisley, right?" She winks.

After lunch I settle into the living room with the television on.

Voices and the occasional laugh waft through from the studio and break my concentration on the soaps I'd started watching. I wish I could muster the courage to simply barge in; but the memory of the room and what had happened in it is still too much for me.

Sunday morning. Monday morning. Tuesday morning. Each day Alexine and Xavier appear on my front step again, itching to get back into my studio. "Honestly, Vi, if I wasn't such a good friend, I'd move in that room and take it for myself," Alexine states one afternoon. "You're going to *love* it."

Wednesday morning, and again they are there, this time with another box of supplies in hand. "Good morning, sunshine!" Alexine sings as they enter the house. "Got any plans for the day?"

I roll my eyes. "Yeah, right."

Alexine smiles. "Fine, fine. Well, you're going to have to hide out in your room most of the day. Sorry."

"What? Why?"

"Because we're moving everything else in and some of it is too big for boxes; you'll see it if you're out here. But then it'll all be done."

Suddenly I don't want to see any of it. "Okay, fine. I'll holler if I need food or something." I shuffle to my room and shut the door. Panic is beginning a slow boil in the pit of my stomach. They will want me to go into the studio today. I don't know if I am ready for that.

I spend most of the day in bed, fighting and occasionally

succumbing to the tears that well up every time I think of that room. I almost wish the CitC folks would show up and take my mind off things, but they've been absent for days now. I wonder if they've finally given up on me. That would figure: just as I was getting used to them and thinking of actually joining them, they'd stopped coming. Just my luck. Sent by God indeed.

Alexine knocks on the door around lunch and announces a McDonald's run. She takes my order, and we all eat in the kitchen— the studio door safely closed. "Another hour and we're through, I think," Xavier says. "You ready?"

My stomach lurches. "No."

Alexine wraps an arm around my shoulder. "We're here, girl. We'll support you. I know it's a big step, but I really think it'll help you."

"I don't see how."

Alexine smiles. "Honey, you've got to start painting again."

"What are you talking about?"

"You've never gone this long without it, right? It's in your blood. You can't just deny a piece of yourself for the rest of your life. It'll kill you. Look at how you've been holed up in here; it's insane! Art will be therapeutic for you. It'll help you heal."

I have my doubts, but it's too late now. The room is almost done, and I can't very well ignore it after all the work my friends have put into it for me. "Look, I'll make use of the room regardless of whether or not I start painting again, okay? But geez—one step at a time."

After lunch I shut myself up in my room again. I feel the panic beating in my chest and try to reason with myself, but I don't seem to want to listen. Eventually I dive beneath the sheets on the bed and turn the radio up loud to drown out my thoughts.

It isn't long before I hear the dreaded sound of someone pounding on the door. I turn down the radio and take a deep breath. "Yes?"

"We're ready!" sings Alexine.

"Well, I'm not."

"Yes, you are, Violette. Come on. Trust us."

Muttering under my breath, I stalk to the door and fling it open, hoping my withering stare will show them I mean business. But they are having none of it. "Give it up, girl," Xavier insists. "We're not leaving till you see this room. And once you've gone in, you can turn right around and dive back into bed if you really want."

"Promise?"

"Promise."

"Now close your eyes," Alexine instructs. Then she takes my hand and leads me toward the room. My feet drag, a physical symptom of the turmoil in my head. *This room better look a lot different*, I think, *because I'm walling it off if it doesn't.*

I can hear the door open, and my heart nearly leaps from my

rib cage. The smell of fresh paint floats around me, and my hands grow cold with nerves. I keep waiting for my feet to hit the wood floors of the studio as my friends shuffle me forward, but it doesn't happen. Something else covers the floor. Curiosity is slowly beginning to get the best of me.

Alexine and Xavier stop propelling me forward and together chime, "Voilà!"

I nearly fall over. I blink once, twice. I try to speak but my voice fails me. I am stunned.

Long ago, I had painted one wall as a view of the ocean, with a beach in the foreground. They ran with that motif and redid the entire room as a beach-house porch. On the ocean wall they had affixed a white porch railing and posts that went up to the ceiling; bamboo shades had been pulled up over the "windows" made by the posts so the ocean was unobstructed. A house front had been painted on the wall facing the ocean, the wall with the door out to the hallway. Windows had been painted on either side of the door, with real window boxes fastened below them and filled with dirt. Bud vases had been planted in the dirt and gerber daisies placed in each one. The side walls had been painted to look as if they were constructed out of slats of wood, weathered by the ocean breeze and water, and bamboo shades had been hung over the window on the right-hand wall. The left-hand wall had another fake window painted onto it, with more bamboo shades. The closet door had been replaced with a shade that went all the way down to the floor, and a real hammock sat beside it with a cotton throw draped over the end of its stand. Even the ceiling got a facelift, having been covered with wood paneling. My easel stood where it always had, facing the fake ocean with the light from the one real window streaming in to illuminate the blank canvas propped on it. The floor had been covered with a jute rug the color of sand.

My eyes fill with tears. I sink to the floor, taking in every detail over and over, disbelieving that this is the same room it had been a month ago. "It's unreal," I finally stammer. "This is unreal. It's beautiful. I can't believe it."

"So, it's a good thing?" Xavier asks.

"Are you kidding?" I laugh. "It's better than good. It's absolutely wonderful!" I shake my head in shock. "Amazing. You guys are amazing."

Alexine plops herself down beside me and smiles. "Believe it or not, there's a little more."

"You're kidding."

"Nope. Open the closet shade."

I scramble to my feet and pull on the cord. The shade ascends to reveal the closet where I'd always stored my materials using the stash-and-dash method (stash the stuff and dash to close the door before it all tumbles out). Now it is filled with shelves and bins, all labeled and arranged according to the materials inside. Propped against one stack of bins is a collection of canvases of different sizes, already primed and awaiting my creativity.

"Oh my heavens," I say simply as I stare. "Oh my."

"So you're all set," Alexine says. "All your paint, all new canvases, your easel, your brushes—they all await your return to the craft."

"I don't know what to say, you guys."

"How about, 'I'll have a new series to you by the end of next month?'" Xavier offers with a wink.

"I think it might take me that long to get started," I admit. "It's been so long, and I don't even have any ideas anymore."

"But you have a notebook of sketches; I saw it when we were cleaning," Alexine says. "I didn't look through it too much because I was afraid it might have private stuff, but I saw some ideas in there that I know you haven't painted yet."

"Yeah," I concede begrudgingly. "But I just don't know…"

Xavier wraps an arm around my shoulder and squeezes. "Take your time, Vi. Just toss some paint up there to get the feel of it again. You can always prime over it."

My eyes are glued to the easel that beckons to me from the corner. "Okay, okay," I finally assent. "I'll give it a try. Eventually."

A week, then two weeks, blur before my eyes. The CitC gang has begun their visits again, having stopped when Alexine and Xavier were there because they didn't want to intrude. I actively engage with them now when they play games or watch movies or eat, but when the praying starts I make myself scarce, usually retreating into the studio to swing in the hammock or stare at the blank canvas Lex propped on the easel the day the room had been revealed to me.

One night they arrive with Pictionary and brownies. We form teams and play for an hour, munching brownies and guzzling milk in between rounds. I find I am actually enjoying myself, and not just because we are playing a game that caters to my strengths. I am feeling social for the first time in months. I am having fun.

They are getting ready to leave and Dana says, "Violette, I can tell you're doing a lot better these days. We've been praying for this." She turns to the others and says, "We should thank God for bringing Violette back." They all agree, and I feel myself reddening. Mumbling something apologetic, I make a run for the studio and close the door, trying to shut out the voices that make their way in from the living room. Just hearing the word *God* makes my hands shake. Acting on impulse, I yank open the closet shade and pull out the bin of paints and brushes. Tossing away the lid, I grab my thickest brush and a jar of black paint, and with just a slight hesitation, I dip the brush into the jar and swipe at the canvas.

A black arc slashes downward from upper left to lower right. Another slash, straight across. Another slash. Another. Globs of paint cling to the edges of the slashes, and I reach out and smear them with the palm of my hand. The coolness of the paint gives me a start; I haven't touched paint in so long I'd forgot the sensation.

I set down the jar with the brush still in it and pick out a jar of red. I scoop some out with my fingers and stroke them onto the canvas over the black. Another jar, this one of deep navy. More slashes and smears and finger-shaped trails. It is quickly beginning to resemble a toddler's finger-paint project—but it isn't the end result that is of interest to me, it is the release.

I stare at the canvas and feel faint. I've been holding my breath for most of the project, reluctant to allow the anger in me too much freedom. For that's what this painting is: a visual representation of how angry I am at God. I reach out and write the letters G-O-D in the mess of paint, then swipe my fingers over it to obliterate as much of it as I can.

A knock at the door makes me jump. It slowly opens, and Dana's head pokes around the corner. "Are you all right, Violette?"

I am embarrassed by the canvas and acutely aware of the statement in the middle of it. Dana sees it and looks to me without any emotion or judgment registering on her face. "You hate it when we pray, don't you?"

The tide I released with the painting is too powerful to hold back. "I hate him. I hate his name. I hate hearing it. I hate thinking it. I was so close, Dana, before…and then he took my husband, and I don't see how he or anyone else could possibly expect me to ever trust him again."

Dana says nothing, merely nods and stands silent while I continue to erupt. "I appreciate what you've all done, how you've all tried to help. Honestly, I'd probably still be in bed if it weren't for you all coming over here all the time and not allowing me to wallow. But…I just can't come back. You understand, don't you?"

Dana shuts the door behind her and sits on the floor against the wall. "I do, Violette. I completely understand. I know what you're going through."

A blackness comes into my mind. "You know," I begin. "Everyone says that like they've walked in my shoes, but until you've actually—"

"I lost a child, Violette."

My mouth snaps shut.

"She was two. Drowned at a backyard barbecue. Ten adults all milling around and no one even saw her slip in."

I am floored. "I… Dana, I'm sorry, I…"

"You didn't know; it's okay. No reason why you should have."

"How long ago?"

"Three years." I begin to stammer another apology, and Dana holds up a hand to stop me. "No one's tragedy is the same as anyone else's, so I'm not trying to say that you'll be like me, or should be like me. But I wanted you to know that I do understand what it's like to have someone taken from you, and what it's like to be mad at God. I'd been a Christian for years, but it didn't matter. I cursed him. I cursed the people that tried to reach out to me. If Jesus himself had knocked on my door, I would have spit in his face."

I am captivated. "So what changed?"

Dana smiles. "God's just as tenacious as we are. He pursued me just as energetically as I ran away."

I scoff, "That's just rude."

"That's love, Violette."

"Sounds more like a stalker."

Dana laughs and stands up. "A stalker has no right to you, but God *made* you. You're just as precious a creation to him as the planet he gave us to live on—even more so, really. He just wants you to love him as much as he loves you." She reaches out to touch my shoulder, and I feel it like a hot coal. "But he will back off eventually if you consistently push him away. The choice is yours."

I stare silently at Dana, drained from my emotional tirade and the months of anger I'd finally let loose. After a few moments Dana opens the door. "Call me, Violette, if you'd like to. Or any of us. We're not going to try to push you into anything, but we do want to make sure you know that God loves you, regardless of how you feel about him. It's okay to be angry, and to doubt, but eventually you'll have to come down on one side or another about whether or not you want to follow him. And regardless of what decision you make, we'll all still love you." She smiles and closes the door behind her, leaving me to stew in my own thoughts and upended emotions.

I sink to the floor after a while, paint the color of dark mud drying on my fingers as I zone out. My mind is working overtime trying to process all Dana has said and the implications it holds for me. If it's true, what she says about God pursuing me and loving me despite the way I feel toward him, then I have to give him credit for perseverance.

"I'm just so tired," I whisper. "I'm tired of being lonely. I'm tired of being angry. I'm tired of being aimless." I speak the words to the empty studio, my eyes transfixed blankly on the ocean mural. "You knew this was going to happen, didn't you? You knew I'd get that close and then get smacked back with this. So why did you allow it?" I don't really expect an answer, but I wait and listen all the same, just in case.

The silence persists, and after a minute I haul my leaden body off the floor and drag myself to the hammock. Rolling into it, not even caring about the mess still on my hands, I curl up and stare at the canvas's hateful composition. The fire that had fueled me to slash through God's name with such vehemence is gone, replaced now by a hollowness that is slowly sucking at my insides.

"I still don't know if I forgive you," I murmur. "That might take a while. Is that all right?" I wait for an answer, hoping this time I'll really get one, and the little patch of peace that suddenly settles in the hollowness serves just fine. It begins to spread like liquid, slipping into all the little nooks and crannies of the hollowness until I almost can't feel it anymore. When I fall asleep, a hint of a smile rests on my face.

*T*ypically Christian came early to the hospital, itching to get up to Violette's room. Today, however, he was still home. Still in his pajamas, in fact, and still sitting at the kitchen table with a soggy bowl of cornflakes before him.

He'd been unsettled since yesterday. Katherine's interest in Violette's and his story had compelled him to tell it, but the next chapter was the one that concerned him the most. It was the chapter that described where they were now.

Four months had gone by before Violette had contacted him again. The first few weeks after their fight had been agonizing. He wanted so badly to call and beg her forgiveness and then take back everything he'd said and promise to do whatever she wanted. All that stopped him was a small shred of rationality that reminded him that a real relationship couldn't be forged when only one partner was willing to be completely committed. It was painfully clear that Violette was not completely committed.

By the end of the first month, it became obvious that she wasn't going to call, that things were officially over, and Christian found himself ready to move on. It had been a frustrating first foray back into the dating world, but he'd learned a good lesson, and more importantly, he'd discovered that he really was ready for a long-term relationship. A part of him would always love Cynthia, but he was ready to let the rest of his heart see some action.

He soon met a newcomer to the church. Her name was Paige, and she was an office manager. She was a no-drama adult, mature and clear about what she wanted in life. They went to lunch after the service and talked about previous marriages—she was divorced—and jobs and their mutual beliefs. She asked him to dinner when they parted that afternoon. He accepted and brought flowers when they met up again two nights later.

They went out a few times before they mutually agreed a certain spark was missing. Their parting was amiable, and Christian didn't feel nearly as bruised as he thought he might.

He chugged along at work and life, looking for new opportunities and considering a European vacation. In fact, he was comparing brochures at the kitchen table when the phone rang and everything changed.

"Hi, Christian. It's…ah…it's Violette."

He almost laughed. "Violette? Well, hi."

"Hey. How are you?"

"I'm fine. You?"

"I'm okay."

"So...what's up?"

A beat of silence passed, then: "Um...I wanted to see if we could maybe get together. For coffee or something. I wanted to talk to you."

"Oh." He hadn't expected that. "Violette, I don't know if that's a good idea."

"W-what? Why not?"

"Because, unless you've had a change of heart, revisiting the past is pointless. I'm not big on the whole 'let's be friends' thing. And I don't think it would be healthy for us—especially me—if we just hung out."

"It's not like that. I promise. Please? Just for coffee."

The desperation in her voice was irresistible. Despite his reservations, he caved. "Well, all right. When and where?"

She was already at the coffee shop when he arrived, sitting at a corner table with a steaming cup of coffee. Her body language screamed *nervous*—tapping foot, crossed arms—and he felt bad that he caused such tension in her. He smiled and gave a little wave before getting in line for his drink, then made his way to the table, hoping his reserved countenance didn't make her feel any worse. He needed to protect himself from being the victim of her emotional roller coaster again, and he was afraid his wariness might show on his face. "Hey, there," he said in his friendliest voice. "Want anything to eat?"

"No, no thanks. And thanks for coming."

He shrugged and pulled out a chair. "No problem. You've got my curiosity piqued; that's for sure."

She laughed a bit and shifted in her chair. Curling her hands around her coffee, she cleared her throat and took a breath. "Um, okay, so here's the deal: I want to get back together."

Christian nearly choked. "What?"

"I want to get back together. I was wrong. You were right. I don't know how else to say it."

He stared at Violette, then his coffee, processing this information. It was the last thing he'd expected. "I...wow. I didn't see this coming at all."

"I know. I'm sorry." The blush he'd always found so adorable was creeping into her cheeks. "I was an idiot before. I mean, I just couldn't seem to let go, you know? And I have now, I swear. I'm over Saul. Well, not over *him,* just over the pining for him and still feeling so attached."

Christian nodded slowly. "Okay. That's good. I'm glad you feel that way. But..."

Her eyes widened. "There's a but?" She clapped a hand over her mouth. "Oh no, you're dating someone. I didn't even think you might be—"

"No, no, I'm not."

She slumped in her chair. "Oh, thank heavens. I can't believe I didn't even... Anyway, never mind. You said but, so what is it?"

How was he going to say this? He rubbed a hand over his face, trying to formulate a response. "Honestly, I'm afraid you're going to flake on me again."

"I can understand that. You have a good reason to think it." She sighed and hung her head a moment, appearing to gather her thoughts. Then she leaned in, looking intent. "I didn't think I'd *want* to be with anyone else ever again. But, Christian, you changed that for me. You...you make me happy. You make me feel safe. You understand the parts of me that long to be understood, and you don't try to change the parts of me that are weird. I need you in my life. And I swear, Christian, I've worked through things. I'm better than I was. Look, we don't even have to say we're dating; we'll just hang out, start from scratch."

She was sincere, of that he was certain. But sincerity didn't translate into healthy. He wanted so badly to say yes, but knew he had to put his own mental health first. "I need to think about it," he eventually answered.

She nodded, the disappointment clear on her face. She gave a small smile. "This feels vaguely familiar, but I think we were on opposite sides before."

He chuckled. "Gives a new perspective, eh?"

She nodded, weariness in her eyes. "Thank you for at least thinking about it. Take your time."

"I will." He leaned across the table and took her hand. "You're an incredible woman, Violette. Regardless of what I decide, I want you to know that. You've got guts."

A corner of her mouth hitched and she said, "Just doing what I've gotta do."

The next day, Christian was finding it difficult to resist the urge to call her and give her a clinical evaluation to determine whether or not she really was as ready as she claimed to be. He knew from his time with Cynthia that it was not wise to put on the therapist hat when dealing with the women in his life; somehow they didn't appreciate being turned into case studies and patients.

His gut instinct was that she needed more time. He had to admit he didn't have much reason to think this, other than the fact that it seemed to be a rather quick turnaround. But who was he to judge? Trust was the foundation of a healthy relationship, and that meant he couldn't be suspicious of her unless she gave him a really good reason to be. He had to take her word for it. And who knows, maybe she really *was* okay. How could he know how deep her issues had been and what she'd done to work on them? Plus, it wasn't like he'd been pressuring her to move on; he hadn't spoken to her in months, and she was the one who left, not the other way around.

If he ignored his gut, the rest of him screamed to take her back. Just seeing her had made him so happy (underneath the curiosity and subsequent shock). He may have moved on, but his feelings for her obviously hadn't dissipated.

Her suggestion of easing back into things was a wise one; he had to credit her with that. She was obviously confident he'd conclude she was ready to commit. Finally he picked up the phone and invited her to meet for coffee again, which they did that evening. Their chat the previous day had gotten them over the awkward first-meeting hurdle, so this time they were both relaxed and eager to catch up. As the hours wore on and the coffee cups collected on the table, Christian came to the conclusion that his gut was either wrong or he was just being ornery. Either way, he wasn't going to give it much thought. He was going to get back together with Violette.

And now here he was, four months later, with the same fears and questions he'd had the first time they started dating. She was definitely more engaged this time around than she had been before, but something in the way she interacted with him still hinted at uncertainty. Sure she was passionate and demonstrative, and not just when he made the first move. But he often detected a slight hesitation in her reaction to his terms of endearment, and she rarely offered any up herself.

Christian dumped the mushy cereal into the disposal and headed for the shower while he stuffed down his slowly mounting concerns about this relationship. He could do nothing about it now, no point obsessing over it. He preferred to channel his energy into willing Violette awake.

Violette

*D*id you remember the ultra-marine?"

Alexine fishes a paper bag from her backpack. "Of course, dummy—I know how you are when you're missing paint. Even food becomes less important."

I grin and shrug with an exaggerated roll of my eyes. "What can I say? I have random priorities."

"Yeah, well, I guess I can understand, especially when you're in the middle of a project. How is it going?"

"Okay, I think. Take a look, it's on the easel."

Alexine peeks in the studio while I continue washing out brushes in the kitchen sink. I've been painting on and off all day, and Alexine has come to take me out to dinner. None too soon, either. It's been more taxing than I thought to work on this project.

His face evokes so many emotions and memories that focusing on it for too long starts to wear on my soul.

"Looks beautiful, Vi," Alexine says when she returns. "I don't see a photo anywhere, though. What are you working from?"

I blot the last brush on an old towel. "My memory. If I'm really stuck I pull out one of our photos—the closeups from the wedding are the best—but for the most part it's all in here." I tap a finger to my temple and smile. "I told him one of these days I'd do it, so I figured it was time to keep my word."

"He wanted you to paint him?"

I laugh. "No, actually, he didn't. But it doesn't matter. I promised to anyway."

Alexine chuckles and follows me into the living room. "Well, when do you think you'll be done?"

"Oh geez, I don't know. I think I'll probably put it away tonight and come back to it later. It's taking a lot out of me, you know? I think it'll end up being one of those when-I'm-in-the-mood pieces."

Alexine's eyes twinkle. "Well, I'm glad to hear your time won't be booked up, because I think I got you a job."

I stop halfway through pulling on a sweater. "Beg your pardon?"

"I was at The Coffee Corner this morning with Donna and June, and I was telling them about the first mural you'd done, and this guy came over and asked about you because he thinks he wants one done in his office."

"Just some random guy?"

"Yeah. Seemed really nice, though. Looked all professional— not a beach bum or anything. I gave him your number."

"You *gave* him my *number*? You gave some *stranger* my number? Are you nuts?"

Alexine holds up her hands in surrender. "I'm sorry, I'm sorry. But seriously, like I said, he didn't seem like a weirdo or anything. He said something about wanting it in his waiting room."

I cock an eyebrow. "Doctor?"

"Wouldn't surprise me."

"Hmm. Well." I finish pulling on my sweater and pick up my purse. "I'll hold you personally responsible if I end up in a Dumpster somewhere."

"Geez, be a little more morbid, please." Alexine socks me on the arm. "Seriously, he didn't look like the ax-murderer type."

"Because they all look like maniacs, right?"

"Hey, I have an idea. Shut up and let's go."

I laugh. "Okay, okay. And thank you. Although I don't know if I'm ready to go back to the whole mural thing."

"You can totally do it; I know you can."

"Well, we'll see."

"Besides, it's a waiting room; how intricate could it be?"

I am studying the canvas, brush poised to paint, when the phone rings. Ignoring the smear of paint on my hand, I grab the receiver and clamp it between my ear and shoulder. "Hello?"

"Um, hello. Is this Violette Corterm?"

The sound of the voice on the other line sends a jolt through my body, and I catch my breath. I stammer, "Y-yes it is."

"Oh, hello, Ms. Corterm. My name is Christian Roch. I met a friend of yours the other day at The Coffee Corner, and she told me about your work as a muralist."

The new client Alexine told me about. Why does his voice send lightning through my skull? "Oh yes. Alexine told me about that."

"Well, I have to admit I'm clueless about how all this works. I'd love to meet you and talk to you about the project, if you're taking new work at the moment, that is."

"Yeah, sure, I'm open to considering it. Why don't we meet at The Coffee Corner, if that works for you."

We decide on a time and say our good-byes. I stare at the canvas after I hang up, lost in thought. After a moment I shake my head to clear the cobwebs and pick up my brush. "You know, babe? I'm kinda nervous about this job," I say to Saul's likeness. "I haven't done a mural in a while." I dab some more and stand back a bit to analyze my work, but I know that isn't the only reason for my jan-gled nerves. "I'll just have to lobby for something simple."

When Christian Roch walks through the door of the coffee shop, my mind is suddenly flooded with images of this man, and myself with him—at the beach, a restaurant, my house, an unfamiliar apartment. Then I hear a voice somewhere—not coming from any-one in the coffee shop, but seemingly in my head. It is Christian's voice, but he's not speaking the words I know he's saying to me as we sit at the table with the photos of my murals.

"Violette, sweetheart, can you hear me?"

I want to clamp my hands over my ears. The sensation is ter-rifying. "Stop!" I yell.

No one in the coffee shop notices my voice, nor does the voice in my head relent. Then, as though watching two movies layered one atop the other, I see myself on a ladder, painting, see myself losing my balance, see myself fall.

$\mathcal{S}$omething was happening.
Violette began to breathe over the ventilator, the pace quickening. Her eyelids fluttered for a moment,

August 15, 2005

and her lips briefly moved. Christian grasped her hand through the bars of the bed. "Violette, sweetheart, can you hear me?" Her hand tightened around his, and he couldn't control the shout that jumped from his throat.

Katherine poked her head into the room. "You okay in here?"

"She held my hand. *Squeezed* it. And her mouth moved."

The nurse gave him a sympathetic smile. "That can happen sometimes. The muscles can—"

"I know, I know. But there's something going on. I know it."

I feel like the universe is falling apart around me. There are too many images, voices, memories vying for my attention. But one thing is becoming clear: none of this is real.

The visions in my mind are so convincing, I feel sure I'll open my eyes and find they are actually happening. But the speed with which they shuffle through my consciousness tells me they can't possibly be. Saul kissing me, Saul's funeral, the empty house, our first meeting—Saul! I desperately want him back. Reliving the memories of our time together reawakens my love for him, and I don't want to let go of those feelings again. Every time his face flashes before my mind's eye, I try to grab onto it, to throw myself into that memory.

But this other voice—Christian's voice—keeps snatching me back to where I am. But where am I? I slowly open an eye, afraid of what I might see.

A hospital room. Christmas decorations, flowers—my appendectomy? But why is it Christian who stands beside me?

Christian watched Katherine disappear back into the hall, knowing she didn't believe him. Regardless of what is common in coma victims, he knew this was something else. This wasn't just random twitches and involuntary muscle spasms. She was waking up.

He grasped her hand more tightly and yanked the chair closer to the bed. Perching on the edge, he began talking, hoping the sound of his voice would pull her back.

"Violette, honey, it's me. It's Christian. I know you're trying to get out of this, sweetheart. I'm here for you. I'll help you. C'mon, sweetie, open your eyes. You can do it, Vi. Open your eyes."

Christian's voice fills my head. "Open your eyes," he's saying. "Open your eyes." They are open, aren't they? No, that doesn't make sense. What I'm seeing can't be real. Christian wouldn't be in this memory. It should be Saul. Where did he go?

"Come back, Violette. Come on, I know you're trying! Come back!"

The voice is getting closer, louder. I feel my grip on Saul, tenuous as it is, slipping. "No, Saul," I beg, "please come back!" I try to conjure any memory I can in the hopes it will bring Saul back to my side. Our wedding, moving into the house, our trip to New York. I close my eyes tight and focus on our wedding, dredging from the depths of my memory every detail I can remember: the color of the flowers, the wind at the beach, the beads on my dress. Then Saul: the linen suit he wore, the corsage on his lapel, the way the wind tossed his hair.

It's working. I can feel the wind, smell the ocean. I carefully plot out each stage of the wedding, willing the movie in my mind to take over like it had before, wanting it to all be established before I open my eyes again.

"Come on, sweetie. I'm right here. You can do it, Vi. Open your eyes."

That voice. It is unrelenting. And every time it calls, I feel myself being drawn toward it—and away from Saul.

Christian wants me back so badly. I can hear it in his voice. He's pleading for me. I have never been good at resisting when people needed me. But if I go to him, I have to leave Saul. *Lose* Saul. Again. Can I do it?

Do I want to?

Her mouth was moving. Christian was beside himself with excitement. This was it, she was emerging, she was coming back! "Come on, sweetie. I'm right here. You can do it, Vi. Open your eyes."

Her hand tightened again on his as her mouth moved beneath the ventilator mask. He reached over with his free hand and gently pulled it from her face. He leaned in close to listen and what he heard made his heart sink. Her voice was barely more than a raspy whisper, rusty from disuse, but the word was clear. "Saul…"

Christian fought not to leave. So there it was. He had his answer. That sneaking suspicion he had tried so hard to ignore had been right all along.

So where did that leave him?

Saul is close. I know it. If I can just ignore that voice, Christian's constant calls to me, I will find Saul again.

Christian is a good man, but he isn't Saul. And that isn't bad, it just *is*. With Saul, I know what is coming. I know where we've been, the arguments we've had, the priceless moments we've shared, and I can stay with him in those memories forever if I can get myself to ignore those desperate pleas for me to come back. If I go back to Christian, who knows what might happen? I might lose him too, and losing one lover is enough for me. Especially now that I have that lover back.

"Saul?" I bring his face to mind, focusing on every detail, and willing the memories to flow and catch me again. "Saul, I'm here." His eyes, his mouth, his chin, his freckles. I organize them into the face I love so much, waiting for a backdrop to form and the movie to start again. In the distance Christian's voice beckons, and I say good-bye to him, wishing him well before shutting my mind to the sound and channeling all my strength and energy into the image of Saul. The voice floats away, and a scene materializes with Saul in the center of my mind's eye.

My relief is almost tangible. Finally. I am back. *He* is back.

An alarm went off on one of the machines standing guard beside Violette's bed. They'd become part of the scenery to Christian. He'd stopped recognizing them as anything but part of the décor days ago. But now it was beeping and flashing, Katherine was elbowing her way between him and Violette, and he, shocked by the unexpected and nerve-jangling sound, staggered back to the wall and stared helplessly at what was happening.

But what *was* happening? Another nurse appeared, then a doctor. They were speaking a foreign language, all acronyms and jargon he couldn't understand. He was forgotten as the line on the heart monitor went flat.

The voices grew suddenly louder, and they were all shouting at each other as they performed their macabre dance around the bed. Katherine started to perform CPR, another nurse raced in and out of the room bringing supplies from somewhere, and the doctor filled syringes and called for the nurses' station to page someone whose name Christian didn't comprehend. Someone in scrubs moved Christian out of the chaos.

Soon he was outside the room, staring in through the window of the closed door, unaware of how much time had passed. Everything ground down to slow motion. The one thing he could see clearly was the heart monitor. The line was flat. When the doctor caught his eye through the window with that look that needed no explanation, Christian turned and stumbled wordlessly down the hall, trying to get away from the room as quickly as he could.

The door to the chapel slammed against the wall with the force of Christian's shove. Tears welling in his eyes, he tripped into a pew and buried his head in his hands. Violette was gone. *Gone.* The enormity of this was beyond his full comprehension. She'd almost come back; he'd seen her waking up not fifteen minutes ago. But now it was all over.

Violette was dead.

"How could you do this?" he shouted. His anger reverberated off the walls and drowned out the nondescript music that played in the room. The week and a half of stress and fear and waiting poured out like a river, and he was overcome with the roiling emotions he'd tried to keep at bay.

You gave me hope. You made me think everything would be okay. You told me what I wanted to hear so I'd come back.

His insides were fracturing, his faith shattering into a thousand bitter fragments. He felt the wall building again—the barrier he'd lived with since Cynthia's death—saw it slowly rising between himself and God. The thought came to him that perhaps this was a test, that God was waiting to see if he'd been serious about coming back to him. He knew their relationship shouldn't hinge on the outcome of Violette's life, but how could he help but base it on that? If God loved him, wouldn't he give him what he wanted?

He ground the heels of his hands into his eyes and swiped away the tears. He'd known this all along, though, hadn't he? He'd known she would die. He didn't get miracles in his life; he never had. Why would now be the exception? His personal history had shown he was not typically the lucky one, and it was the lucky ones whose lovers came out of comas and lived with them happily ever after.

Besides, it was clear what would have happened if she *had* lived. *Saul.* The one word she'd uttered since her fall, and it was the name of a man he, Christian, could never live up to and never replace. Maybe that's why God had allowed her to die. He was sparing Christian from the pain of knowing she was out there, somewhere, and just didn't want to be with him.

He sat in the pew, numb, unaware of time, staring at nothing and letting his mind wander. He didn't think about what would happen now with Violette. He'd let Alexine and Xavier take care of it; they'd known her longer than he had. He didn't dwell on what had just happened; it was all too surreal to think about right now. He just stared.

The sound of the door opening startled him from his day-dreaming. A middle-aged man walked down the center of the chapel and up to the altar, where he knelt, crossed himself, and then stood and began to straighten up the candles. A priest. Christian watched him as he tidied the altar and then removed a white handkerchief from his pocket to wipe down the carved wood. He moved to the other side of the altar and was now facing Christian, who tried not to stare. The priest nevertheless looked up and smiled at him. Christian nodded in response.

"Is there anything I can do for you?" the man asked.

"My girlfriend just died."

The priest tucked the handkerchief back into his pocket and descended the stairs, shaking his head. "I'm so very sorry," he said. "May I pray for you?"

"If you'd like."

"Are you a believer in the Lord?"

"That's sort of up for debate right now."

The priest nodded in understanding as he sat in the pew in front of Christian. "It's not easy to see through heaven's eyes at times like these."

"You'd think it would get easier each time it happened."

The priest's eyebrows arched. "Ah, so you've been here before, have you?"

"My wife, a few years back. Cancer."

Again he shook his head. "What a terrible blow."

"Huh. I suppose you could say that."

They sat in silence for a few minutes, until the priest suddenly stuck out his hand. "Father Tom, by the way."

"Christian," he replied, shaking the hand and smirking slightly. "An ironic name at times like these."

"Ah, ironic, yes—or prophetic, the way Bible names were. Like Simon's name being changed to Peter, because he would be the rock of our church. Perhaps God knew you'd need the label eventually to help you stay the course."

"Well, I wouldn't have a problem if he'd just stop being such a sadist and messing with my faith. Pardon my language."

"Trust me, I've heard much worse. You could say nothing that would offend me. Now, in what way is God, ah, being a sadist and messing with your faith?"

Christian took a moment to sort everything in his mind. "When my wife died," he began, "I blamed him. I've been angry with him ever since. And then I met Violette—my girlfriend—and everything was going so well. Then she fell off a ladder and went into a coma, and I was so afraid I'd lose her too. And one night I sort of had it out with God, and I truly believed he promised me everything would be all right, that it would all turn out okay. I had hope again, because I thought that was God promising me Violette would be okay." Christian shrugged and slumped back in the pew. "But apparently not."

The priest listened, eyebrows knit in thought, and Christian felt compelled to let him off the hook. "Listen, I'm not expecting you to pull me out of this, so don't feel bad if you don't know what to say. Or if I just don't care what you say." He flashed a quick smile and the priest did the same.

"I'm just the messenger, Christian. I don't take it personally if you don't respond. That's God's role. Now, this Violette. Was she a believer in the Lord?"

"Yeah, she was."

"And do you think she is now in heaven?"

"I suppose, yeah."

"What would her life have been like if she had come out of the coma?"

"No one knew. The doctors said she could be fine, but she could also be a very different person. There was just no telling."

"So perhaps God was giving you hope that Violette would be well again, which she now is if she is with him."

Christian barely nodded, not wanting to admit that made some sense. "Perhaps."

"It is a messy, fallen world we live in, Christian. Many times in my life I've wished the Lord thought me ready to come home so I could stop dealing with it. Don't mourn for her death. Be happy for her, that she's out of a world full of pain and ugliness and living now in a world of indescribable beauty."

A world of indescribable beauty. The ideal world for an artist, all right. Think of what she could paint there. Christian caught himself smiling. "She was an artist. She'd definitely appreciate the beauty of heaven."

The priest's face brightened. "There you go! Unencumbered by earthly materials—think of what she could create with inspiration like that. Especially," he continued, his countenance sobering, "if God knew she wouldn't create again in this world."

Christian hadn't thought of that. What if she'd emerged from the coma unable to paint? She would have been miserable. She wouldn't have been the Violette he loved, though he would have continued to love her anyway. But she wouldn't have been the same person.

"So maybe he spared her by taking her?"

"It is certainly possible."

Christian stared at the stained-glass windows he'd hoped to show Violette one day. Now she was seeing the real Jesus, not just the fragmented and imperfect mosaic of glass in the wall. How could he begrudge her that? And how could he be angry with God for giving her that opportunity without insisting she first go through life unable to do the one thing she loved most?

The priest stood and clapped a hand to Christian's shoulder. "I'll leave you to your thoughts," he said. "I will be praying for you, though. Take care, Christian."

"Thank you, Father."

With a final squeeze, the man slipped out of the pew and out the door.

Losing Violette versus having a Violette who couldn't paint. If God had given him the choice, would he have had the strength to deny himself and give her up for her sake? Obviously he couldn't know for sure that was the life she'd have been faced with if she'd lived, but it had been a possibility; the doctors had been up-front about that from the start.

He wanted to think he'd have loved her enough to put her happiness before his. They would have both been miserable if she'd been unable to do the one thing she was so passionate about. At least, by letting her go, one of them would be happy. And knowing she was in a perfect world could make him happy, on some level.

And Cynthia was there too. He'd never thought about that before. His wife and his girlfriend hanging out in paradise. He wondered if they'd compare notes about him.

So where does that leave us? He looked at the cross on the wall behind the altar, sensing God was waiting for Christian's final verdict. Could he begrudge God for putting Violette out of her misery? Could he fault him for wanting to spare her a life of frustration and pain? Certainly he could think of better ways God could have chosen to remove Violette from the world—falling from a ladder didn't seem particularly merciful—but the result was the same, and it could have been worse. Just as Cynthia had been lucky, in a way, not to have to endure months or years of agony. He'd never thought of it that way before; he'd been too caught up in how quickly it had hit and how bereft her death had left him.

"You win," he finally said, his voice flat with resignation, grief, fatigue. "I have to trust that you knew best what Violette needed. As much as I hate it, as much as it hurts, I think I am willing to bow to your expertise."

He sat in the chapel for a while, soaking in the silence that enveloped him. Then he stood and made his way back to Violette's room to say a proper good-bye. He was coming out of the elevator on her floor when Alexine came tearing out of Violette's room. "Where have you been?" she gasped. "Do you know what happened?"

"I'm sorry. I was in the chapel. And yes. I was here when it happened." He wrapped his arms around her. "I'm so sorry, Alexine."

Alexine pulled away, eyes shining. "You *don't* know, do you?"

"Know what?"

Saul's hand reaches out for mine, and I take it gratefully, following him into the light that is shining behind him. This isn't any memory, though. Where am I?

"Saul? What's going on?"

He doesn't speak, only smiles at me and pulls me forward. He stops before a figure—a man, I think, but I can't see the face—and I realize the figure is the One radiating the light that fills the space we are in. Then Saul lets my hand go and steps away. "Saul! No, come back!" An overwhelming emptiness sucks at my soul as he walks beyond me and the figure of light. He is moving toward what looks like a building, but in a form and style I've never seen before. I notice other people in the distance, and a towering gate that glistens like a multicolored diamond.

I turn back to the figure, unsure of what to do, and it reaches out a hand to me. Its wrist is pierced, a black hole in the center of the light. Awareness fills me in an instant, and I drop to my knees before my Savior, speechless, Saul forgotten.

His hand rests on my head for a moment, and I am filled with an overwhelming sense of love and warmth and calm. Then he speaks. "Not yet."

Before I can ask what he means, everything begins to recede at breakneck speed as I am pulled backward through a tunnel, watching the light shrink away to nothing.

Silence.

Cold.